# DOCTOR WHO
## AND THE
## CURSE OF PELADON

# DOCTOR WHO
# AND THE
# CURSE OF PELADON

Based on the BBC television serial by Brian Hayles
by arrangement with the British Broadcasting
Corporation

## BRIAN HAYLES

### Illustrated by Alan Willow

Number 13 in the
Doctor Who Library

A TARGET BOOK
published by
the Paperback Division of
W. H. Allen & Co. Ltd

A Target Book
Published in 1974
By the Paperback Division of W. H. Allen & Co. Ltd
A Howard & Wyndham Company
44 Hill Street, London W1X 8LB

Reprinted 1976
Reprinted 1980
Reprinted 1982
Reprinted 1984

Printed and bound in Great Britain by
Anchor Brendon Ltd, Tiptree, Essex

ISBN 0 426 11498 1

# Contents

# I

# The Deadly Guardian

The electric storm clawed and tore its way across the night sky like a wild animal, flaring suddenly into ripples of lightning more eerie and majestic than the three moons of Peladon. The harsh wind, drowned only by fitful claps of ragged thunder, howled and keened through the crags and passes of Mount Megeshra while, far below, deep-shadowed valleys and canyons echoed and re-echoed to the almost continuous shudder of sound. Yet another blaze of light flowed across the torn sky, silhouetting the mountain peak. A mighty granite-stoned castle became starkly visible before slipping back into the darkness, its pointed turrets challenging the night. It was the Citadel of Peladon.

Inside the castle, thick walls reduced the wind's sound to a chilling moan. On the walls, torch flames dipped and guttered fitfully as Torbis, Chancellor to King Peladon of Peladon, strode purposefully through the shadows along the corridor leading to the throne room. His lean face grimaced as he shrugged himself deeper into his heavy cloak. At his age, every winter seemed colder than the last. But this year would be a famous landmark in the chronicles of Peladon—and part at least of the glory would be his, Torbis, Chancellor and mentor to the young king.

A growl of thunder reached him from outside, and he scowled. It was a black night, worst yet of the winter storms and Hepesh, High Priest of Peladon, would make the most of it. Although younger than Torbis by ten years, Hepesh held stubornly to the past, scorning the future, foretelling its doom by omens. No wonder the aliens called Peladon barbaric. The past was important, but it had to change, to evolve—and Torbis was determined that it should happen soon.

As Torbis approached the great doorway to the throne-room, the guards standing there brought their ornate pikes up to attention. Torbis casually acknowledged their salute. The guard commander moved to open the throne-room doors, and Torbis glanced idly upwards at the massive statue set on the balcony over the entrance. With a small habitual gesture, Torbis acknowledged the stern image : a cruelly stylised rendering of Aggedor, the Royal Beast of Peladon, by tradition the spiritual guardian of the king. The chiselled face stared back sightlessly. Without giving further thought to the grim stone guardian, Torbis strode forward to meet his royal master.

Seated on the throne, Peladon watched affectionately as Torbis advanced and bowed his grizzled head in formal greeting. It was obvious that the old man was pleased. Peladon had good reason to share his pleasure. In spite of the well-meaning resistance of Hepesh, the High Priest, who now stood beside the throne, the promise that had once been no more than a dream would soon become reality. Peladon made a simple gesture of welcome. Torbis relaxed and stepped closer to the throne. His glance took in the two figures standing there : Grun, the King's Champion, superbly muscled, impassive and ritually mute; and Hepesh, whose dark eyes scarcely hid his quiet hatred.

Hepesh raised a richly-ringed hand to stroke his beard. His glance flicked away from the Chancellor's gentle face to that of the pale, handsome youth on the throne. He so resembled his warrior father in physique and bearing. But, because of the added graciousness and warmth of his mother the Earthwoman, the boy lacked the auto-cratic manner of the great kings of the past. Yes, she was the source : breaking the royal bloodline, and planting the seeds of change not only in her son and Torbis, but in the minds of the whole Grand Council. She was dead now. Hepesh and Torbis had, as Regents, brought Pela-don to his throne when he came of age, and he still sought

8

their guidance and wisdom. There was still a chance that he could be persuaded—but time was running short.

Torbis spoke, proudly. 'The delegate from Alpha Centauri has arrived, your majesty. We wait only the Chairman delegate from Earth.'

'There is no point in wasting time,' said Peladon crisply. 'Alpha Centauri will present his credentials to me as soon as possible, tonight.'

Hepesh stepped forward, tight-faced and sharp-voiced. 'Your Majesty—think again! This folly—'

Torbis turned on Hepesh, but spoke calmly.

'This folly as you call it, Hepesh, has been discussed and decided in Grand Council. You have had your say there and you were outvoted. Accept that decision!'

'Hepesh,' interceded Peladon, 'this meeting with the Commissioners of the Galactic Federation is only a preliminary discussion—nothing more that that . . .'

'You have been misled, majesty—' retorted Hepesh earnestly. 'Torbis and the fools who support him seek to discard the ancient ways of our people!'

'Superstition and ignorance may be the tricks of your trade, priest,' snapped Torbis, 'but they are no foundation for a glorious future!'

'A future in slavery to aliens?' questioned Hepesh coldly. 'Such a denial of our great traditions will surely bring the curse of Aggedor upon us!'

'Perhaps Aggedor has more faith in his people than you, Hepesh . . .' growled the old Chancellor.

'The storm outside these walls has raged ever since the first alien landed on our planet,' asserted the High Priest. 'The omens cannot be ignored!'

Peladon stood, slight but commanding. 'Torbis— Hepesh!' His young face was stern. 'End this brawl!'

The old Chancellor stepped back from Hepesh reluctantly.

'Omens . . .' he muttered. 'It will take more than superstition to frighten me!'

'The spirit of Aggedor protects the throne,' Hepesh observed acidly. 'Do you deny his power?'

Torbis made to answer but turned to find Peladon standing between him and the High Priest. The two older men fell silent as the young king placed a restraining hand on each of them. His face carried rebuke—and the reminder of past friendship.

'Friends . . .' he said, quietly, 'you have been more to me than councillors or regents. Both of you—in your own ways—have been my father since his sad death . . .'

Torbis studied Hepesh deliberately, but his words were for the king. 'My only allegiance is to the throne,' he said.

'Then end this hate between you . . .' begged the king, 'for my sake . . .'

The old Chancellor turned his tired face to Peladon, and nodded. 'All I ask is that you do not forget your trust,' he murmured, 'or my teaching . . .'

Always the politician, thought Hepesh bitterly, as Torbis bowed before the king.

'Torbis,' said the young king, 'I shall not betray you—or my people . . .'

Hepesh could not remain silent. 'But your majesty—'

Peladon quelled him with a glance. 'Hepesh, there is no more to be said. If the Committee of Assessment judges us favourably, this planet will join the Galactic Federation. I expect your help to that end.'

Peladon paused, his eyes searching the High Priest's face for the response he demanded. 'Well?'

Hepesh said nothing, but bowed his head in silent agreement. The king was a child no longer; he must be obeyed. Peladon, satisfied, turned to Torbis, who stood with an air of quiet triumph.

'Bring the delegate from Alpha Centauri to me in formal audience, Torbis,' commanded the young king; and with Hepesh and Grun at his side, watched the Chancellor bow and depart from him.

Once outside the throne room, Torbis move to effect the king's order with the deliberate dignity of his ancient rank. No one would have guessed at his elation. Inwardly his pleasure was immense; the king's assurances mean almost certain success for Torbis' plans. The clums attempt by Hepesh to delay the Committee of Assessment had failed. The bubble of superstition had been burst, and the young king had freely taken the bold step out of barbarism towards a new, magnificent future. Federation technology would mean that cultural and social advances normally taking a thousand years could now be achieved in less than a century! A new Peladon, stronger, more sophisticated, more civilised . . .

Torbis stopped, suddenly, the dream wiped from his mind. A deep, throbbing howl rang out in the shadows of the corridor, and terror gripped the old man like a vice. He could neither turn nor run; and as he stood, immobile, that terrifying cry sounded again, closer now and more menacing still. What he next saw made Torbis gape with terror and fall to his knees, defenceless. 'Aggedor!' he gasped, cringing too late from the mighty claw that with one crushing blow struck him lifeless to the ground.

.    .    .    .    .

In the throne room, that dreadful animal howl had brought an immediate reaction from Hepesh. 'Aggedor . . .' he whispered hoarsely, glancing towards the young king who, like Hepesh and Grun, stood frozen in alarm at the blood-curdling cry. At the second cry, Peladon was already moving towards the corridor, but Grun, his Champion and protector, ran swiftly before him in the direction of the danger.

Hepesh tried to hold Peladon back, speaking urgently to him: 'Majesty—no! The danger is too great!'

Peladon shook himself free, and moved to follow Grun, now far ahead. 'It is Torbis who is in danger! Save him, Hepesh!'

With a warning glance over his shoulder, Hepesh ran ahead. Peladon, now escorted by his guards, lagged only a few paces behind.

Sword in hand, Grun quickly came upon the crumpled body of Torbis—but what he saw there stopped him in his tracks. Few things could strike fear into Grun's heart.

'Aggedor!'

To him, death on the battlefield was nothing. Now he moaned with wordless terror, letting fall his sword and covering his face abjectly before the shadowy, majestic being that stood menacingly over the body of Torbis. One glimpse of that savage, white-tusked head was enough —not even Grun, mightiest of Peladon's warriors, could raise his sword against the Royal Beast and live. Then, as the King's Champion grovelled before him, the vengeful cry echoed through the castle once more, and, with a flicker of shadows, Aggedor was gone.

At the sound of approaching feet, Grun stood, shaken by what he had witnessed and, desperate to explain. Hepesh threw Grun only a cursory glance, then knelt by the body to check for any signs of life; there were none. Drawing the old man's cloak over the sightless face, Hepesh looked up at Peladon, and shook his head.

'Torbis . . . dead?' whispered the young king, his face drawn with suffering. 'But how—why?' He turned to Grun, his eyes fiercely questioning. 'Grun—what happened?'

Puzzled, he watched as Grun knelt pathetically before him. He saw the intense fear which haunted the warrior's face. Grun pointed to the nearby cast-metal torch holder. It was formed in a hideous representation of the Royal Beast. Knowing that Grun, though mute, would only tell the truth to his king, Peladon turned anxiously to his High Priest.

'Aggedor . . .' said Hepesh, grimly.

He rose to his feet from beside Torbis' body, and studied his young master with bitter dignity.

'His spirit has risen,' he declaimed. 'The ancient curse of Peladon is upon us. We are doomed . . .'

# Into the Chasm

The fury of the storm was increasing. The ceaseless flow of lightning across the sky threw the rocks and crags of Mount Megeshra into savage relief against the wind-hounded shadows. Into that maelstrom of noise was pitched another—grinding, mechanical, unnatural . . . and a shape unlike anything that had ever been seen on the planet Peladon. Suddenly, solidifying out of thin air, a chunky, dignified blue box fell victim to the wind's claws. It lurched ominously, coming to rest on a rocky ledge poised over the chasm below. Heavy though it was, the strange box perceptibly moved, each time crushing against the brittle edge of the rock, and making its position yet more precarious at every moment. The wind, as though seeking to throw back this alien intruder, howled and screamed all the louder.

The interior of the blue box made nonsense of its drab outward appearance. Instead of what an Earthling of the 20th century would recognise as a police telephone box, its interior space was unlimited, and styled with an elegant futurism. At its centre stood a cylindrical complex of controls and monitoring equipment that would do justice to all but the most advanced spaceship; but the hands that operated the controls belonged to a tall, slightly theatrical figure, his exuberant shock of white hair topping a lean but humorous face, which smiled with boyish pleasure. He flipped one final switch, and the protesting mechanism groaned to a halt. His companion, her natural prettiness made even more beautiful by the evening dress she wore under her cloak, was less amused.

'There you are, Jo,' said the Doctor. A perfect landing —well . . . nearly, anyway . . .'

'And about time, too,' muttered Jo, impatiently.

The Doctor smiled benevolently, studying the controls with evident pride.

'It's alright for you to grin,' pointed out Jo with irritation. 'Here am I all dolled up for an evening on the town with Mike Yates—'

'And very pretty, too,' complimented the Doctor, his eyes still checking the dials and gauges of the control panel.

'You are infuriating, sometimes!' exclaimed Jo. 'Why I let you talk me into coming for a joy ride in this thing, I don't know!'

The Doctor looked pained. 'Not a joy ride, Jo . . . This is an occasion—the TARDIS' first test flight since I got it working again!'

Jo couldn't stay angry with the Doctor for long. Her face softened and she touched his arm as a sign of truce. 'You and your toy,' she smiled, shaking her head as though to a naughty child. 'But it's me that's going to be late, you do realise that, don't you!'

'My dear Jo,' comforted the Doctor, 'we'll have arrived back only seconds after we left—if not sooner. This is the TARDIS, you know—not a number 88 bus!'

Jo moved to the doors, obviously keen to be on her way to her evening date. She turned and smiled at the Doctor, expectantly. 'That's alright, then,' she said brightly. 'If you'll just open the doors and let me out . . .'

But it wasn't going to be as easy as that. Jo knew it as soon as she saw the Doctor hunched over the controls, his boyish face totally enthralled by the sheer enjoyment of putting the TARDIS through its paces again.

'Routine landing procedure first, Jo . . .' murmured the Doctor, assimilating the variety of information offered to him by the telemetric displays. 'Atmosphere . . . gravity . . . magnetic field . . . yes, all normal. Now—let's see what the videoscanner tells us . . .'

At the door, Jo waited with growing impatience. The Doctor flipped a switch and looked across the master viewing screen. It was completely blank. Jo gave a little sigh. 'Precisely nothing,' she said, glaring at the Doctor's rear view as he dived under the control console and started groping amongst the mechanism there.

'Aha!' he cried, reappearing and waving a small piece of electronic equipment at Jo. 'It's the Interstitial Beam Synthesizer on the blink again!' He saw Jo's face, and hurriedly stuffed the gadget into his pocket, sheepishly. '... but I'll fix that later ...'

Something about the Doctor's face troubled Jo, and a tiny flicker of apprehension brought a frown to her eyes.

'We *are* back at Base ...' she asked the Doctor, 'aren't we?'

'Of course we are,' the reply came back with a beaming smile, 'and it was a perfect landing.'

The words were barely out of his mouth when the TARDIS gave a sudden shudder, and then an abrupt lurch. Jo was sent helplessly spinning against the control console, and from there bounced into the Doctor, who also had been thrown off balance. They steadied each other, but it was far from easy. The TARDIS was now at an angle well out of true.

'You did say ... perfect,' Jo gulped, trying not to look alarmed.

'Oh, everybody makes mistakes, Jo ...' quipped the Doctor. But his face was grave.

The TARDIS shivered, and shifted again. The frown on the Doctor's face grew deeper, and Jo clung to his arm even more tightly. Something was wrong!

'Doctor ...' she piped quaveringly, 'are you *sure* we're back at UNIT H.Q.?'

Holding on to Jo with one arm, the Doctor reached out with his other hand and operated the control switch that would open the doors to the world outside.

'There's only one way to find out, Jo,' he said grimly, completing the operating circuit and moving towards the doors. 'You stay here. I'm taking a look outside ...'

But this was more easily said than done. As the doors opened, the devil-wind outside ripped and roared its way into the TARDIS, making it vibrate with its fury. It was all the Doctor and Jo could do to stay on their feet.

Opening the doors had been easy. Getting to them and

outside was altogether more difficult. But as the Doctor slowly fought against the swirling wind that now drove into the TARDIS, his movement towards the door seemed to steady the tilting balance of the craft. Until he stepped outside, that is. Then his weight—the prime balancing factor against the desperate tilt of the floor—was removed, and the TARDIS leaned even more alarmingly. Jo, her evening cloak fluttering and flapping about her, could only cling to the control panel helplessly.

'Doctor!' she cried plaintively, '. . . where are we . . . ?'

Outside, the Doctor was applying all his weight to the lower edge of the TARDIS's door frame, desperately trying to hold the balance against the shuddering windblast. He took a deep breath, sized up the situation and decided he didn't like it in the least. The ledge on which the TARDIS was resting may well have been a mountain track once—now it was little more than a narrow shelf of crumbling rock. It needed very little more to send the blue box toppling down to the chasm below. There wasn't a moment to lose.

The Doctor spoke calmly, but with a deliberate authority that Jo knew better than to question. 'We've got ourselves halfway up a mountain, Jo . . .' he called back into the TARDIS, forced to pitch his voice above the shriek of the wind. 'The TARDIS is balanced on the edge of a rock shelf. Just don't sneeze, that's all . . .'

Jo could just see the Doctor's face, and she answered bravely to his reassuring smile. 'What do you want me to do?'

'When I tell you to move, move—but *gently*. Understand?'

She nodded, and hoped the Doctor couldn't see that she was shivering. She concentrated on what he was saying, and her fear receded a little as she acted out his commands.

'Down on your hands and knees, then . . . That's it. Now—move towards me . . . slowly.'

For a moment as she crouched, Jo could no longer see the Doctor and her heart leaped into her mouth. But she found that her new position took her out of the whiplash of the wind, enabling her to crawl towards the door reasonably easily. Her eyes were fixed on the Doctor's hand stretched out towards her. Then, almost within reach, she slipped—and the TARDIS shuddered. In that brief moment of panic, Jo flattened herself against the floor, heart pumping furiously.

'Come on, Jo!' The Doctor's voice, low and urgent, made her look up. His hand was reaching for hers, only inches away—but her panic paralysed her. She couldn't move.

'Very gently, Jo . . .' murmured the Doctor, the calmness in his eyes giving her strength. 'Give me your right hand . . .'

Willing herself into motion, Jo reached out. Just as her hand touched the Doctor's, the TARDIS moved again. She closed her eyes tight, and gripped hard.

Still his voice was there, calm and clear. 'That's it . . . now the other hand . . .'

Her eyes now fixed on the Doctor's face, Jo brought her hand into his confident grasp. For a moment, locked together at arm's length, they breathed and listened tensely to the rumble of disintegrating rock outside.

Then, taking all Jo's weight, the Doctor leaned hard backwards and rapped out the command : 'Pull yourself out—now!'

In a flurry of wind-whipped dust and rocks, Jo was outside, falling on top of the Doctor, all of a heap—but safe. Breathless, she saw the Doctor staring past her. When she turned, the TARDIS was gone. She looked back at the Doctor in dismay. Then, realising that she too could have been swept down to the awful rocks below, she heaved a shuddering sigh of relief. The Doctor gave her shoulder a reassuring squeeze, then moved past her to the rock edge. She crawled up to his shoulder and looked down. Kneeling there together, they watched the tumbling fall of the bizarre blue box as it vanished into the echoing shadows, far beneath them.

Jo gasped with horror. 'It'll be smashed to bits!'

The Doctor drew her back from the edge, gently. 'No it won't, Jo,' he said patiently. 'The TARDIS may have its faults, but it *is* indestructible . . .'

'After a fall like that?' Jo couldn't believe it. 'It's hundreds of feet down—you can't even see the bottom!'

'Our real worry,' observed the Doctor thoughtfully, 'is how to get to it from here . . .'

Jo looked from his frowning face to the chasm at their feet. She shivered.

'It's impossible,' she said.

A sudden gust of wind ruffled the Doctor's hair, and he narrowed his eyes against its sting. 'I'm afraid you might be right, Jo . . .' he mused.

Jo followed his gaze as he tried to follow the line of the broken path, upwards. As he looked, an even brighter flash of lightning than before lit the crags above them. The Doctor's face grew alert, and he pointed upwards, urgently. Jo looked too, but had to wait for the next lightning flash before she could see the grim castle which topped the mountain peak far above.

'I think we'll go and ask for help . . .' said the Doctor, brightly.

'Up there . . . ?' exclaimed Jo in dismay.

'Somebody must be home,' remarked the Doctor drily, 'unless you have a better idea?'

'But we don't know who they are,' cried Jo, 'or even where we are. We could be anywhere!'

The Doctor tested his first foothold. 'Exactly!' he declared. 'And we won't find out any quicker, hanging about out here in this weather, will we?'

She stared at him aghast, the wind whipping her cloak about her. 'You don't mean . . . we've got to climb?'

The Doctor smiled at her, reassuringly. 'Once we reach a regular pathway, it'll be easier. You'll see, Jo.'

She smiled weakly, and tried to put the memory of the falling TARDIS out of her mind. 'After this,' she shouted above the storm, 'Everest will be simple!'

And, boldly, they began to climb.

The tragedy of Torbis' death loomed like a hovering bird of prey over the citadel; but Peladon knew what he had to do. He had made a solemn promise to the old man, and he would keep it. The killing, whatever the real reason behind it, must not be allowed to destroy the dream for which Torbis had fought with such determination. As the body of the Chancellor was being richly prepared for traditional burning, Peladon was sending Hepesh to complete what Torbis had set out to do: summon the latest alien arrival for formal presentation to the king. Hepesh had been almost sullen in his reluctance, but the king had insisted. To stop the process now would be worse than a defeat; it would put back the clock by a hundred years. Torbis had been right—the time was now. On that, Peladon was determined.

'The delegate from Alpha Centauri, Council member of the Galactic Federation, presents himself before you, King Peladon.'

The formal words of Hepesh's announcement failed to hide the unease he felt at the alien being which was standing by his side. Tall as a man, but single-footed like a sea anemone, its iridescent turquoise body was discreetly covered by a cloak emblazoned with its Galactic rank. From beneath the cloak rippled six tenuously graceful tentacles. The whole was surmounted by an octopod head containing one huge yet strangely beautiful eye. Due to gravitational differences the body of Alpha Centauri found swift movement difficult, but the tentacles were capable of sensitively mimed expression. They rippled politely as Peladon spoke. 'Peladon welcomes the delegate from Alpha Centauri . . .'

The young king's face was grave, betraying no wonder at this, the third of the aliens so far arrived. The others were no less unusual in appearance, but they were intelligent and their mission was sincere. When Alpha Centauri spoke, however, Peladon could barely conceal a smile. For the voice that came from the shimmering hexapod was as shrill and elegant as a nervous lady-in-waiting. In spite of the authority invested in the alien, the effect was almost comical. Even Hepesh raised an eyebrow as he listened to the alien delegate's formal response.

'As a member of the Preliminary Assessment Commission, I have great hopes that your planet will be acceptable as a candidate for the Galactic Federation,' piped the exquisite voice. 'A magnificent future could be yours . . .'

'That is my sincere hope,' said Peladon. Then indicating Hepesh, he continued, 'Hepesh, my acting Chancellor and High Priest, will give you every assistance in your mission.'

The six tentacles indicated their acknowledgement. Hepesh tried not to flinch from their moist and gleaming gesture of friendship.

'We willingly accept the . . . hand of friendship,' the High Priest said diplomatically. 'The glorious future that you speak of will be given consideration . . .'

'You will realise,' fluted the hexapod alien, 'that there are certain necessary conditions to be met.'

'The King's Grand Council will examine your demands,' Hepesh said with deliberate coolness.

'My formal coronation will not take place until we have achieved Federation Membership,' offered Peladon warmly. 'That is the extent of my personal commitment.'

'Your majesty is obviously sincere,' trilled Alpha Centauri, 'and I have little doubt that we shall quickly decide—'

'Unfortunately,' interjected Hepesh with cold logic, 'our discussions cannot begin until the arrival of the Chairman delegate from Earth.'

'He will be here soon, Hepesh. Earth is many light years from us. Is that not so, Alpha Centauri?' said the king.

'Indeed, your majesty,' the alien replied, mildly disparaging, '—a remote and unattractive planet, I believe.'

'The fact remains,' retorted the High Priest, 'that the Earth delegate is not here. The omens are not good!'

Peladon could see the anger boiling behind Hepesh's eyes, and sensed the outburst that was to come. He leaned forward, his hand raised in admonishment, but Hepesh was not to be denied. 'Your majesty ignored my warning before,' insisted the haughty priest, 'and now Torbis your respected Chancellor lies dead . . . slain by the wrath of Aggedor!'

'Hepesh! Enough!' snapped the king, and the High Priest fell silent. But his words had had effect. Alpha Centauri's tentacles rippled uneasily, their colours changing to a milky blue in sure indication of alarm.

'You speak of death . . . Is there danger here?' queried Alpha Centauri. 'Such a state of affairs is not acceptable to the Commission!'

'It is an internal matter,' Peladon replied soothingly. 'There is no reason for the delegates to be troubled.'

'But your Chancellor *has* been killed . . . ?' insisted the hexapod nervously. 'An atmosphere of violence is not suitable for a balanced assessment!'

'The circumstances were . . . mysterious—but the truth will be brought to light,' asured the young ruler. I assure you that there is no danger to you or to your fellow delegates. The Commission can continue with perfect safety.'

The tentacles became less agitated, and their colour became almost normal once more. Alpha's voice too, dropped to a less hysterical pitch as the king anxiously awaited the reply.

'Naturally,' murmured the hexapod, 'I accept your majesty's assurances . . .'

'Do not condemn us for being ruled by our ancestors,' begged the king. 'We have many primitive traditions that must seem strange to you . . . but we are willing to learn.'

With a small gesture, Peladon indicated that the audience was at an end. Hepesh bowed and moved towards the throne room doors.

'Chancellor Hepesh will escort you to the delegates' meeting chamber,' the king said, quietly dismissive, and settled back on to the throne. Alpha Centauri turned gracefully and followed Hepesh out. But Peladon's eyes, as he watched them go, were dark and deeply troubled . . .

.    .    .    .    .    .

The path leading up the mountainside was growing increasingly steeper. Negotiating the narrow, boulder-strewn way was made no easier by the cutting, swirling wind, and Jo was desperately tired. The Doctor seemed to have limitless energy, and frequently half-carried Jo over the more impassable sections—but they seemed nowhere near to reaching the mighty castle set high above them. Coming to a wider, scrub-covered ledge, Jo leaned against the rock face in an attempt to escape the wind and get her breath back. Seeing her tired face, the Doctor came back to her, and shielded her, sympathetically. Her hair, wisping into a wild parody of the elegant style Jo had set it in for her dinner date, added to the strain in her face. She looked upwards, past the Doctor, then back into his face and shook her head.

'It's no use, Doctor. I can't go any further. I just can't.'

The Doctor tried to coax her gently into continuing. He knew the dangers of exposure on a mountainside in weather like this. 'I know it's tough, Jo . . . but you're doing fine.'

'I've nearly broken my neck getting *this* far!' she complained miserably, and she slumped back against the rock face, near to tears. But the Doctor's determined face showed he would make no concessions and his voice was equally purposeful.

'Well, we can't go back. And we can't very well stay here all night, can we? We'll take a breather and press on.'

The breather was only a short one; but it gave Jo enough time to pull herself together and make a further effort. By the time she was ready to go on, the Doctor had scouted their situation and come up with a plan.

'The path has crumbled away further up—we'll have to traverse along this ledge and find another way, that's all,' he decided. 'I'll take a look on this side. Stay here, Jo, will you?'

Jo was only too happy to rest for a moment longer, and tucked herself into a corner of the rock which was partly protected by a dense patch of scrub. When the

Doctor returned she was nowhere to be seen. His features tightened in alarm. What had happened?

'Jo—!' he shouted against the howl of the wind. 'Where are you? Jo!' He glanced at the edge of the rock shelf, and for a sickening moment wondered if Jo had been swept over into the chasm far below—then the sound of her voice made him turn with relief to the rock face behind him.

'Over here, Doctor!' came Jo's excited voice. At first, he couldn't see any sign of her. Then, from the side of the clump of scrub, her tousled head looked out at him, bright-eyed and smiling.

'It's a tunnel—behind this bush,' she cried. 'Come and see.'

As soon as he was inside the entrance of the tunnel, the Doctor knew it was out of the ordinary. For one thing, it should've been in total darkness—but it wasn't. Jo was much too pleased to be out of the wind that still howled outside—though it was barely audible now.

'I just fell into it!' she bubbled exitedly. 'Isn't it super?'

The Doctor didn't answer immediately. He was examining a broad vein of phosphorescent rock. It was giving off enough light to disperse all but the blackest shadows. Jo, watching him, suddenly realised that the tunnel was not merely a sanctuary against the wind—it was manmade, and it had to lead somewhere.

'Doctor . . .' she ventured, 'I don't like it.'

The Doctor was already tracing the line of faint light farther down the tunnel. Jo followed him, hastily.

'Fascinating . . .' he murmured, then paused and pointed out to Jo that the walls were only partially natural.

'I know,' she said, 'I can see. But who did it?'

'Carved out of the living rock,' mused the Doctor. 'Clumsy, but effective. And this band of phosphorescent strata . . . That's ingenious!'

'It's also very peculiar,' muttered Jo, keeping close to the Doctor's shoulder. 'Have you even seen anything like it before?'

'Can't say that I have, Jo ... no ...'

'And that storm outside—didn't you notice anything odd about that, too?' asked Jo, urgently.

'In what way?' muttered the Doctor casually, his mind more taken by the quality of the rock formation.

'Well ... all that sheet lightning and thunder and wind —but no rain?'

'And what,' queried the Doctor, 'do you deduce from that?'

'Nothing,' said Jo, trying to sound casual. 'It's just that I wonder if we're still on Earth. That's all.'

The Doctor stopped examining the rock, and turned to look gravely into Jo's wide-eyed face. He didn't smile.

'As a matter of fact, Jo, you may be quite right.' He turned his head to look along the dimly lit tunnel which wound its way deeper into the mountain. 'I think we'd better try and find out, don't you?'

. . . . .

The delegate's conference room was, like the rest of the mighty castle, walled with faced stone. In spite of its rugged quality it was luxurious by Pel standards. Four alcoves contained iron-hinged wooden doors leading to the living quarters reserved for each alien. The walls between these alcoves were hung with richly woven tapestries bearing the Royal Arms. In the lower quartering of each tapestry featured in gold, was a stark representation of Aggedor, the Royal Beast. Wall torches lit the room cheerfully, and another, smaller alcove contained the statue of a huntsman, cast in a metal like bronze. Alpha Centauri was used to more elegant and sophisticated surroundings. His sensory system flinched slightly at the primitive impact made by the chamber. Politeness however prevented his commenting on the barbarism of the style and content of Peladon's hospitality. 'Very suitable,' piped the iridescent hexapod rippling his tentacles in appreciation.

'Our ways are different from yours, naturally,' mur-

mured Hepesh, assuming correctly that Alpha Centauri
was used to something better. 'If there is anything further
that you wish . . .'

'A question,' fluted the hexapod, its solitary eye con
fronting Hepesh at uncomfortably close range. 'Why wa
your Chancellor destroyed?'

'That is for the king to explain,' replied the High Pries
evasively, then quickly changed the subject. 'This chambe
is for delegate meetings. Your personal living quarter
are here.' He opened one of the alcove doors. The hexa
pod looked inside, mentally flinched at the harshness c
the decoration, and turned back to Hepesh to make
suitably bland comment. Before he could do so, a fla
metallic voice cut across the room.

'Greetings. I am the delegate from Arcturus. Who ar
you?'

Alpha Centauri had never before met an Arcturian fac
to face, and what he now witnessed made his sensor
tingle with curiosity and apprehension. At first glance h
saw a tinted but transparent globe of fluid, mounted o
a compact and elaborate traction unit, the whole strongl
resembling a robot rather than an alien life-form. Bu
closer examination showed that within the fluid floate
a delicate, multi-strand organism, and that at its centr
was lodged the vital neuro-complex that governed it
actions. Alpha Centauri's admiration for the design an
elegant complexity of the life-support unit mingled witl
an indescribable feeling of unease. Something told hir
that Arcturus was dangerous. It would pay to take care

'The delegate from Alpha Centauri,' announce
Hepesh, as politely as his distaste for both aliens woul
allow.

'Greetings, delegate Arcturus,' said the gleaming hexa
pod. 'Have you heard about the incident? A cour
official has been killed.'

Inside its globe, the delicate organism grew agitated
its surrounding fluid darkening ominously. 'If there ha
been violence, we could be in danger,' rapped out th
clinical voice. 'Hepesh—explain!'

26

'An internal matter, delegate Arcturus,' answered the High Priest. 'Do not be concerned . . .'

'We are on a planet alien to our own life-form snapped Arcturus, 'therefore we are bound to be concerned for our own safety. Self-preservation is of vital importance!'

'Members of the Federation,' explained Alpha Centauri with appropriate tentacle movements, 'are committed to the rejection of violence.'

'But,' grated Arcturus chillingly, 'we are capable of self-defence when necessary. Observe!'

Hepesh and Alpha Centauri watched, slightly puzzled, as Arcturus turned to face the statue in the far alcove. With a cold click, a panel on the front of the creature's life-support unit opened, revealing the stub of a normally concealed weapon. Small in scale, it seemed innocuous— until it fired. Then, with a spit of electronic power, the pencil-thin beam of laser light flashed out. Within a split second, the statue glowed, then disintegrated. Hepesh remained impassive, but there was fear in his eyes. Alpha Centauri flushed deep blue with disquiet and was happy to see Arcturus' deadly laser gun retract and click shut again.

'Be warned,' Arcturus cautioned. 'Do not provoke us!'

Hepesh bowed politely and moved to the door. Before leaving he turned and said with dignity, 'We desire only your friendship.'

.     .     .     .     .

The deeper Jo and the Doctor went into the mountain, the darker the passage became, in spite of the natural light from the strange streak of phosphorescent rock. The Doctor, leading carefully, suddenly stopped. Jo bumped into him and clutched his arm anxiously. 'What is it?' she whispered, straining her eyes to see what lay ahead. She could detect nothing.

'It's a light, Jo,' murmured the Doctor. 'It could be a door. Gently, now . . .'

But the light falling into the passage a little way ahead

was not a door. As they crept closer to the source, they saw it plainly for what it was: a window guarded by a carved stone grille. Still wary, they peered into the chamber beyond, and Jo gave a little gasp. Inside the grille, she glimpsed a small room containing an altar. Over it hung a mask, carved, hideous yet proud, into the living rock. Jo got her breath back and stared at the carving, fascinated. Her forehead pressed against the stone bars that kept intruders at bay. The Doctor looked thoughtful and said nothing. Neither of them knew that they were looking on the face of Aggedor.

The stark simplicity of the inner chamber was strangely impressive. Jo turned from looking at it, to question the Doctor. She could tell that he, too, was impressed.

'Doctor,' she murmured, 'what is it? Some sort of shrine?'

'Yes,' agreed the Doctor, 'it could well be, Jo.'

'Is that the god, then?' asked Jo. 'Or is it a demon? I've never seen anything like it before. Have you?'

'No, I haven't.' The Doctor paused, then frowned. 'Not on Earth, at any rate . . .'

Jo looked sharply at him. She understood just what he meant. Not on Earth! Then where *were* they? The Doctor didn't give her the chance to ask the question.

'Let's move on, Jo,' he said, and walked forward into the tunnel which loomed ahead. Jo quickly ran after him. Within the space of a dozen paces, they had stopped again. Ahead of them the tunnel forked, and neither the right nor the left branch offered greater hope of freedom. Jo looked up at the Doctor's brooding face and wondered what he was thinking.

'Eeny, meeny, miney, mo,' recited the Doctor, as though in answer to Jo's unspoken question. Then, with a beaming smile, he gestured grandly towards the right-hand fork, implying that Jo should lead the way. Amused, Jo dropped a quick curtsey, and turned to lead on—but instead of moving forward, she flung herself against the Doctor's chest in desperation. For, out of the depths of the right-hand path, came the ringing, bestial howl of Agge-

lor. As Jo buried her face against him, the Doctor stared
aard past her. He could see nothing but darkness beyond.
Once more that terrifying cry rang out, closer now and
vith more menace. At last the Doctor moved, bundling
Jo forward quickly.

'This way, I think, Jo,' he muttered, and half-running,
hey took their chance on the left-hand path.

# 3

# An Enemy from the Past

Peladon was alone. He had sent Grun the Faithful from
him, and Grun, although unable to put thought into
words, had understood Peladon's deep need for solitude.
The young king's thoughts were all on Torbis and the
years past that he had spent guiding and teaching the
boy who would one day be king. It had not been Torbis'
ask alone : Hepesh, too, had played his part. Until the
coming of the aliens, the two men had been as one : uncles
to the young charge who had been placed so trustingly
in their care by Ellua, the boy-king's Earthling mother.
Was Hepesh right? Had she betrayed them into a new
slavery? Peladon rejected this without question. Hepesh
was a creature of the past. Peladon's mother had been
blessed with a rare vision. What she foresaw must come
true.

One particular memory drifted into his mind; the day
when, accompanied by his mother, Hepesh and Torbis,
Peladon had been brought to the throne room and told
he meaning of his coming of age. He had refused to sit
upon the throne, and had insisted that it could belong only
to his illustrious father, the dead king. But Torbis had
lfted him up and gently set him on the throne, and
Hepesh had spoken gently to him, telling him what was to
be . . . The words still echoed in his mind, proudly.

'*Though the royal blood that flows in your veins ha*
*mingled with that of strangers, you shall be Peladon o*
*Peladon, greater than your father, greater than any pas*
*or future king . . .*' Hepesh's intoned words had echoe
clearly around the throne room walls. His mother ha
smiled and taken Peladon's small hands, placing th
right in Torbis' lean grasp, and the left in the softer
jewelled hand of Hepesh. Together, they had made a
boy into a king.

But now Torbis was dead. The coronation would be a
empty ritual without him, although his task would b
so near to completion once the young king was anointe
and crowned. Now he was king-elect, and not all-power
ful; then he would be ruler with total power. Hepesh, th
High Priest of Aggedor, was held in high esteem through
out the land. Peladon would need to lean heavily on hin
in the daily running of the affairs of the kingdom. Onc
there had been complete trust in the two men wh
guided him; now, Peladon's mind was filled with ques
tions. Should he remain committed to the Federation, o
was this the moment to reconsider? Was the death c
Torbis a black omen, as Hepesh claimed? Pelado
suddenly became aware that he was no longer alone. H
looked up and frowned. Hepesh was standing before hin
as though summoned by the questions in Peladon's mind
The king did not hesitate to speak.

'Why was Torbis killed, Hepesh?' he said, his voic
tight with emotion.

'Torbis saw your future as a servant of the Galacti
Federation. That was wrong. I—and your people—se
you as the independent ruler of a glorious kingdom.'

Peladon frowned more deeply. The answer was no
complete—Hepesh was using formal words to hide facts

'And do you believe that he was destroyed by Aggedor?

Hepesh replied smoothly, without pause. 'It was ,
terrible warning. We dare not ignore it!'

Another evasion, thought Peladon. He leaned forward
sharp-eyed, determined to wring a clear-cut answer fror
the older man. 'The Federation delegates are here at m

royal invitation,' he said pointedly. 'Why, then, was it not I who was struck down?'

Hepesh remained unshaken. 'It was Torbis' blind advice that swayed you. It was his folly that would have destroyed you—and your kingdom. He would have made you a slave, not a king.'

'Hepesh, it was you that told me, just as Torbis did, that a king must choose—and choose courageously,' cried Peladon. 'I made that choice!'

The High Priest inclined his head, acknowledging the implied rebuke, but his reply was firm; 'Aggedor has shown us the true way ...'

Peladon could control his anger at the old man's stubbornness no longer.

'Backwards, into superstition?' he snapped, his eyes blazing. 'Hepesh—it was you that taught me to fight, to ride—and to think! Help me to realise my dreams!'

Hepesh did not answer, but met his young lord's gaze with impassive dignity. Peladon's hand gripped his shoulder.

'I know what is best for my people,' said the king.

The priest, unflinching, spoke with a quiet intensity. 'And I do not trust the aliens!' he said. 'I will not let them lead you into a trap!'

Peladon drew back, and exclaimed icily, 'They have been open and honest with us, Hepesh.'

It was the priest's turn to show anger now. 'To them, we are no more than savages! They despise and distrust us!'

'Then I will talk to them, freely, to remove all suspicion from their minds,' retorted Peladon. 'Summon the delegates!' The old man did not move, but the sharp disapproval on his face did not deter his master.

'*Now*, Hepesh!'

Peladon watched the High Priest leave. The massive doors closed after him. The young king had already made a decision: if Hepesh intended to hold back, it was time to seek new allies.

Hepesh did not go immediately to do the king's bid-

31

ding. Outside the throne room doors, he encountered the mighty Grun, King's Champion, and a dark plan began to form in his mind. Acknowledging the guard's brisk salute, Hepesh motioned Grun to his side. He drew him to the corner of the corridor only a short distance from the throne room entrance. Grun's loyalties were traditional : to Peladon, to Hepesh, and, most of all, to the spirit that ruled the throne—Aggedor. As the defender of that throne, Grun would act—ruthlessly if necessary—to preserve his king. But clearly, he was not yet aware of the danger of the aliens. It was time for Hepesh to teach him.

'Grun,' murmured Hepesh, and paused before continuing to study the handsome rugged face, 'you have been honoured.' Grun stared back at him, not fully comprehending the High Priest's purpose in taking him aside. Hepesh contrived to place himself between the King's Champion and the statue of Aggedor that surmounted the throne room entrance, then spoke on, quickly and purposefully.

'You have seen the face of the living Aggedor—and yet you have been spared ! It is a sign . . .'

Grun's eyes instinctively sought the great stone statue which was set on the high balcony. When his eyes met those of Hepesh, they revealed awe—and fear.

'I am the holy servant of Aggedor,' continued the High Priest, 'and it is for me to interpret such a sign. It is for *you* to act, if so ordained. Is this the truth?'

Grun nodded; and behind the stern mask of his face, Hepesh smiled. He held the key to Grun's utter obedience.

His ornately ringed hand clasped the metal-studded wristguard of the warrior's light armour, and he moved closer, his voice an urgent whisper. 'You know the legend —the ancient Curse of Peladon—you know what it means, Grun?'

Grun nodded seriously as Hepesh's words thrust home. 'Our kingdom is in danger, Grun . . . and with it, our king. You are his protector, and it is to you that Aggedor has given a warning of his displeasure. He knows the future, Grun. He sees it as we cannot, and he is angry!'

The mute warrior swiftly nodded in agreement. But Hepesh had not finished. 'That future, Grun. Who brings the new future to us?' Grun's glance flicked down the corridor in the direction of the delegate's chambers. Hepesh nodded; Grun understood.

'Yes, Grun—those aliens are strangers to our great traditions. They blind the king with golden promises, but they bring only danger and mistrust!' Hepesh stared hard into Grun's eyes. 'They are our enemies, Grun—enemies of the king, and of Aggedor. They must be . . . dealt with. But cunningly. Do you understand?'

He looked over his shoulder at the great statue which loomed over the doorway to the throne room. Grun followed his gaze, then looked back into the High Priest's eyes, knowing what he had to do. Hepesh nodded, satisfied, and offered his holy ring, a huge jewel carved into the form of Aggedor's face. Grun knelt, briefly, pressing the ring to his lips then against his broad forehead, accepting Hepesh's blessing for the task that he must now perform. He stood and saluted formally, as the priest moved quietly away on his own errand.

'I go to summon the delegates to the king's presence, Grun. They will come this way shortly. Think only of this—' Hepesh threw one last glance at the grim-faced statue, 'Aggedor has spoken . . .'

.        .        .        .        .

The eerie cry of the unknown threat behind them had not reached the Doctor and Jo for several minutes now. Their pace had slowed considerably. The vein of phosphorus light had virtually dwindled to nothing and in the gloom, the rock-scattered floor had made walking dangerous. Suddenly a welcome glow appeared ahead.

'It's a torch,' Jo cried excitedly. 'Doctor, can you see? Civilisation at last!'

'Yes,' the Doctor agreed, rubbing his chin and brooding, 'but a rather unusual one. Look at the holder, Jo. It's the equivalent of the Renaissance on Earth—the late Middle Ages.'

33

'They could just be antiques.' offered Jo hopefully. 'Let's get on. I don't like this tunnel.'

The Doctor finished examining the metal torch-holder, and looked further along the tunnel. It bent to the right, and from the curve came the flickering glow of what appeared to be other torches. He took Jo by the elbow, and moved onward. Neither of them noticed that the floor was smoother now—not ridged and rough-hewn, but laid with flagstones.

'Come on then, Jo,' smiled the Doctor, 'I've a feeling that we're coming to the end of it at last . . .'

It wasn't until they turned the corner that they realised how right the Doctor was—the tunnel ended in a blank, man-made wall. Jo turned to the Doctor, her face miserable with despair.

'We're trapped,' she said plaintively. 'All this way, and it's a dead end!'

'Don't be so sure, Jo. Don't you notice something rather . . . unusual?' observed the Doctor drily.

'Apart from the fact that we're very probably stuck in the middle of some freaky planet in the Dark Ages, no.'

'It's the torches, Joe . . .' indicated the Doctor. 'If this tunnel is never used, why are they alight?'

'A brilliant deduction, my dear Doctor,' grumbled Jo wearily, 'but you still haven't told me how we get out!'

The Doctor moved to the torch nearest the end wall of the tunnel and fumbled with it as he muttered half to himself. 'They were an ingenious lot of fellows in the Middle Ages, Jo . . . Got up to all sorts of tricks. Ah, yes, I thought as much!' With a low groan, the wall swung open—and they were inside the citadel.

.        .        .        .        .

Alpha Centauri was restless. The unaccustomed austerity of the castle was not exactly soothing to the nerves of a Galactic civil servant. The primitive surroundings didn't seem to effect Arcturus, but Alpha Centauri felt obliged to complain anyway.

'These backward planets,' the hexapod sighed despondently, 'so uncivilised . . . no atmosphere purifier . . . no protein dispensers.'

The thin rasp of Arcturus' metallic voice brought no comfort. 'This is a diplomatic mission,' came his reply, 'not a holiday!'

'A Galactic official deserves *some* consideration at least!' twittered the octopod-headed alien. 'And have you *seen* the colour scheme in my living quarters? They obviously have no idea what 'peaceful' means!'

'We are here,' rapped out the Arcturian delegate, 'to bring order and political unity to this planet—not to decorate it like a Centaurian fun-palace.'

Before Alpha Centauri could think of an effective reply, the door opened. Standing there was Hepesh, cold-faced and haughty. Both Arcturus and the mildly agitated hexapod swung round to confront him, but he wasted no time in casual greetings. 'King Peladon sends greetings and requests your immediate presence in his throne room,' he announced.

'Does this mean that the Earth delegate has arrived at last?' grated Arcturus, moving towards Hepesh.

'Not yet,' replied the High Priest, addressing himself to the quivering organism within the tinted globe.

'But we cannot proceed without our Chairman!' protested Alpha Centauri, tentacles rippling in vague alarm.

'This is an informal meeting requested by his majesty for personal reasons,' blandly replied Hepesh, turning abruptly to lead the way out. He checked at Arcturus' sharp voice.

'The delegate from Mars—'

'He has been informed,' said Hepesh brusquely. 'He and his assistant are on their way to the throne room now. You will follow me there. The king is waiting.'

.        .        .        .        .

The entrance to the secret tunnel was concealed behind an ornate tapestry, and it took Jo and the Doctor a full minute to extricate themselves from its heavy folds. Looking about, they found themselves in a deep alcove set off from the broad main corridor. With a quick glance, the Doctor took in the manner of building, its style and rather heavy aspect. It confirmed his earlier guess, and he smiled at Jo rather smugly.

'Definitely an emergent civilisation, Jo. Probably with strong ties to an earlier, more barbaric hierarchy.'

'That makes all the difference, of course,' remarked Jo, sarcastically. 'All we need is King Arthur and his knights!'

'Wrong period, I'm afraid Jo,' smiled the Doctor, 'and this certainly isn't Camelot. Rather fine castle, though, don't you think?'

Jo shrugged, and followed the Doctor as he paced forward into the deserted corridor. 'Let's try this way,' he said, brightly—but Jo wasn't listening to him.

'Doctor!'

He turned. Her face was full of alarm. Then he, too, heard the noise . . . a heavy, shuffling stride, overlayed with a rhythmic hissing sound. Jo pulled the Doctor into the shadows of the alcove. Neither of them spoke, but huddled there listening intently as the eerie noise drew nearer . . . nearer . . . and at last came into sight. Jo's eyes, wide with fright, could barely smother a gasp of horror; even the Doctor grew tense at what they now saw.

It was a biped, but totally unlike any other walking creature Jo had seen before. Its massive feet shuffled along as though dragged down by heavy weights. Its huge hands were like crude, stub-fingered clamps. It was entirely covered with an armoured skin that was ridged and plated like an alligator or prehistoric reptile. Its helmet-like head showed a lipless, scaly-skinned lower jaw that seemed to struggle desperately to draw in air from the atmosphere about it. Set in the terrifying head were two blankly menacing eyes, screened as if by perspex. Moving as relentlessly as a battle tank, it strode past them down the corridor and out of sight.

'Doctor . . .' murmured Jo weakly, 'what *was* it?'

The Doctor's face was grim, as he replied, 'That, Jo, was an Ice Warrior . . . product of the planet Mars!'

'You've met them before?' asked Jo wonderingly.

'Yes. And they aren't very pleasant company,' replied the Doctor, drawing back the tapestry that hid the concealed door. 'This is no place for us. Back to the tunnel—come on!'

But the wall was closed. The Doctor was so intent upon finding the catch that would release the secret door and allow them to escape, that he barely noticed the sound of the approaching guards—until it was too late. He turned to find himself, like Jo, pinned against the wall by a ring of ornate but vicious pikes. This time, there was no escape. Jo caught the Doctor's look of resignation and agreed with him.

'Alright,' she sighed. 'Let's give ourselves up. At least this lot look human . . .'

. . . . .

In the throne room, the delegate Arcturus and Alpha Centauri had taken their place before Peladon, who with Hepesh and Grun flanking him, patiently awaited the last delegate to join the group : Izlyr the Martian, and his lieutenant Ssorg. When the Martians had taken their place, the guards closed the great doors behind them. Peladon observed Izlyr as he aproached the throne and greeted the king. Where Ssorg was massive and brutal, Izlyr was sharply elegant. His helmet head revealed his rank; his speech and physical presence spoke without doubt of the martial tradition which had formed him. Although documented as officially representing the Galactic Federation as an agent for peace, every inch of him bore the hallmark of the warrior class. He spoke with icy precision.

'We are here at your request, King Peladon. Address us.'

Peladon nodded graciously and, with a gesture, greeted the assembled delegates. He spoke without formality. He knew it was imperative that these aliens believe in his sincerity. If they did not, everything was lost.

'Thank you for your attendance,' said the young king pleasantly. 'By now, you know of the tragic incident involving my Chancellor, Torbis. Since his sad death, it is Hepesh, my High Priest, who acts as my administrator. The loss was a personal one. Torbis was more than my adviser; he was a trusted friend.'

'But he was killed,' stated Izlyr coldly. 'Why?'

Before Peladon could answer, Hepesh stepped forward and spoke. As High Priest, Chancellor, and acting regent, he had this traditional right. But Peladon's eyes flashed in quiet anger as Hepesh boldly addressed the aliens.

'The death of Torbis was a supernatural warning—!' he cried. Before he could continue, Peladon interrupted.

'Hepesh offers a personal opinion, not mine. He claims this tragedy is connected with one of our more ancient legends—'

With a faint whine of his traction unit, Artcurus skimmed forward slightly and gave voice. 'Your priest speaks of a warning. Perhaps it is more than that.'

'It is a superstition—nothing more!' exclaimed the young king, 'It has no bearing on the purposes of your committee. You must understand that!'

'On the contrary,' hissed Izlyr, 'the incident could represent a meaningful threat—to us, and to the Federation.'

'But it was Torbis who died,' insisted Peladon earnestly. 'This legend concerns my people only!'

Alpha Centauri was agitated but not yet hysterical. 'Your ancient legend seems rather violent and unpleasant ... and rather too convenient.'

'Its timing disturbs me,' agreed Izlyr. 'Explain this legend to us—now!'

Hepesh looked towards the young king with the merest hint of challenge in his eyes. The royal youth was powerless to refuse. He nodded grimly. With a bold gesture, the High Priest indicated the tapestry behind the throne and, on it, the representation of the Royal Beast, Aggedor.

'It concerns the Royal Beast of Peladon,' he declaimed

38

with quiet authority, 'a creature now extinct, but once the fiercest of all wild beasts on this planet. Only young men of noble birth would hunt him to prove their courage. His fur was so rare that it was used to trim our royal cloak and the coronation crown. And it is his majestic head that is our royal symbol.'

Alpha Centauri muttered an aside to Arcturus, making sure it did not reach the throne. 'These are such barbaric practices . . .' The hexapod sighed, its sensors trembling at the thought of such a violent creature.

'Mighty is Aggedor,' continued Hepesh in the voice he used in the main for religious celebrations and state ceremonies, 'and it is written there will come a time when the spirit of Aggedor will rise to warn—and to defend—his royal master, Peladon. For, at that time strangers will appear upon the face of the land, bringing peril to the king, and dreadful tribulation to his kingdom.'

The eyes fixed on the High Priest suddenly saw him falter. His eyes stared past the assembled group towards the doorway. For a moment, he showed an unease rarely seen upon his face. The others turned to see what had disturbed him so deeply. Standing there surrounded by armed guards, was the Doctor, with Jo at his side. Even by the humanoid standards of the Pels, Jo and the Doctor looked unusual—it was as though by speaking the legend aloud, Hepesh had brought part of it alive. Peladon stood, surprised and intrigued by the new visitors. His gaze fell most intently upon Jo who, in spite of her recent ordeals, managed to look elegant and beautiful. And it struck both Peladon and Hepesh that this Earth-alien had the face and form of Ellua, long dead.

In his turn, the Doctor stared intently at the strangely mixed gathering about the simple throne, and his eyes narrowed as he saw the commanding figure of the Martian warlord move towards him. The Ice Warrior they had seen earlier stood close by his shoulder. Jo tensed at the menacing approach of the grim pair, and the Doctor tried to reassure her.

'It'll be alright, Jo . . .' he murmured, as she glanced

The Doctor stared intently at the strange mixed gathering about the simple throne

appealingly towards him. At his words, she tried to smile. The warlord came to a crisp halt directly before the Doctor. Then, with a swift, imperious gesture, he first struck his own left shoulder with his clenched fist and offered his open gauntleted hand in greeting to the Doctor.

'Chairman delegate from Earth—greetings!' said the warlord with chilly formality. 'Delegate Izlyr, sub-delegate Ssorg.'

The Doctor managed to acknowledge the greeting with suitable dignity. The other aliens now approached. Jo edged closer to the Doctor, and tried not to shudder at the bizarre parade of alien forms before her : the massive and threatening Martians, then something that looked like an operatic octopus—she lost track counting the tentacles —and, finally, a travelling goldfish bowl with a nasty-looking creepy-crawly swimming about inside. It was all too much ! Like the Doctor, however, she concentrated on being sociable; at least their arrival hadn't turned out to be too unwelcome. None of those in the throne room noticed the discreet withdrawal of Grun, the King's Champion, as he moved stealthily from behind the throne to the half-concealed doorway that gave access to the balcony over the door outside.

'Delegate Alpha Centauri,' piped the gleaming hexa-pod, waving its tentacles excitedly, 'the Galactic Committee is much in need of your experience and judgement.'

'Delegate Arcturus,' clipped out the mechanical voice of the floating neuroplasm. 'You are late.'

'My apologies to the Committee,' the Doctor replied quickly. 'My space shuttle . . . a forced landing, on the mountainside. I'd like something done about recovering the machine.'

It was Hepesh who stood before the Doctor now. His face was haughty and his voice coldly suspicious. He made no gesture of greeting, and he seemed to be deliberately avoiding the presence of Jo.

'The recovery of your space vehicle will be arranged,' he said. 'I am Hepesh, High Priest of Peladon. Protocol

41

demands that you formally present your credentials of office to King Peladon. Hand them to me.'

Hepesh thrust out his hand. The Doctor could only gesture apologetically. 'I'm sorry. That isn't possible,' he said. 'You see, we lost everything in the crash.'

Hepesh didn't look as though he believed this impromtu explanation, but before he could question it, Peladon spoke out from the throne.

'We can deal with the protocol later, Hepesh. Present the delegate from Earth, and his companion.'

Hepesh was not to be denied all formality, however. He glanced at Jo's slightly rumpled hair, then questioned the Doctor sternly. 'I assume this female is of royal blood?'

Jo couldn't help smiling at the thought, but as she made to deny the mistake, a small gesture from the Doctor kept her silent.

'My dear chap,' the Doctor addressed Hepesh cheerfully, 'what makes you ask that?'

The High Priest's arrogant expression showed how much he despised the ignorance of this new alien.

'You are standing within the Citadel of Peladon,' he explained. 'This throne room is royal and most sacred. Each guard is of noble blood, and each seeks to uphold the honour of his king. Only such men of rank, and females of royal blood, may set foot here . . .' He paused, meaningfully. 'The penalty for trespass . . . is death.'

Jo was not to be kept silent any longer, but what she said next made the Doctor raise his eyebrows in surprise.

'Doctor—' she exclaimed regally, dismissing Hepesh with a sweeping wave of the hand, 'I refuse to deal through intermediaries. Kindly present us to your royal host!'

For a moment, Hepesh was rendered speechless by Jo's words. The Doctor stepped in quickly.

'Yes, of course,' he muttered hastily, then moved forward past Hepesh to the foot of the throne, Jo's hand resting on his with regal condescension. 'King Peladon— as Earth delegate, I greet you. May I also present Her Royal Highness Josephine, Princess of . . .' For a brief

42

second he floundered, 'Princess of Tardis!'

Jo curtseyed deeply, while the Doctor bowed. Peladon indicated that they should rise. His words were addressed to them both, but his eyes were fixed on Jo. He could see now that she was not as he first thought, a living reincarnation of his mother, Ellua the Earth Princess. But he had seen how even Hepesh had been startled by the uncanny resemblance to portraits of his mother as a young woman. To those who believed in omens, this beautiful visitor *must* point to good fortune!

'Greetings, Princess,' said Peladon, smiling warmly. 'I'm sorry that your long journey ended so uncomfortably.'

Jo smiled at the young man who sat before her. He might be a king, but he certainly wasn't stuffy or snobbish, for all the splendid clothes he wore. He must be about my age, Jo decided. Handsome, too. And as he was being so friendly, she could afford to be one up on the Doctor for a change. After all, she was a Princess—*he* was a mere Doctor!

'The whole business was quite deplorable, your majesty.' She threw a half-glance at the Doctor, then, continued. 'The pilot was unfortunately rather inefficient.'

The Doctor looked at Jo indignantly, but could say nothing. In any event, he was still trying to work out just what he—as Chairman delegate from Earth—was doing on the planet Peladon in the company of these other aliens. Still, at least the king seemed friendly enough. Perhaps, the Doctor thought wryly as the king continued to address Jo, a little too friendly for the High Priest's peace of mind.

'I'm glad it was nothing more serious,' said the king. 'You bring a welcome beauty to a solemn occasion.'

Jo was pleased with the compliment. 'Thank you, your majesty. You're very kind.' At the same time she was uneasily aware of Hepesh's cruel eyes, boring into the back of her head. She concentrated on Peladon.

'As you may know, my mother was an Earthwoman,' continued the king.

The aliens, not understanding the significance of this

43

apparently trivial conversation, fidgeted, restlessly. No one noticed that one person was missing—Grun.

The King's Champion had by now reached the top of the short stair that gave access to the balcony over the throne room doors. He paused, lithe-footed and silent as a cat, for all his burly strength. From behind him, the voice of the king mingled with those of the aliens. Soon they would come out into the corridor below. He must be ready for them. Underneath his ornate perch, two guards stood impassive and unhearing. They must know nothing of what he was about to do. The simple instruments that he would need lay waiting behind the great stone statue of the Royal Beast. Grun made the holy sign of obedience and set about his task. Even with the block of stone as fulcrum and the metal bar as a lever, it would not be easy. But Grun's mighty strength would do the rest, when the time came to act.

Jo had turned from the throne to face Izlyr.

'Princess, what is your power on the Committee of Assessment?' he asked.

The Doctor knew that Jo had even less idea of the purpose of the aliens Committee than he did. He answered for her quickly.

'The Princess is present,' he said affably, 'as a royal observer. We felt the situation called for it.'

Izlyr understood and was satisfied. 'Ah, I see,' he commented with a brief nod. 'As on my planet, you still preserve the aristocratic process . . .'

'Yes,' observed the Doctor, 'in a democratic sort of way.' He returned Jo's little smile of gratitude.

Arcturus, however, was not particularly pleased.

'Chairman delegate,' rapped out that metallic voice, 'we are not here to indulge in social diplomacy!'

'Er—no . . . of course not,' mumbled the Doctor, still without knowing the purpose of the Committee. Fortunately, Arcturus provided the answer.

'Our purpose is to consider admitting this somewhat backward planet into the Galactic Federation.'

'Thank you for reminding me,' replied the Doctor, his

mind on Izlyr. What was an Ice Warrior warlord doing on a Committee such as this? Alpha Centauri's fluting voice broke into his thoughts.

'Unfortunately, the success of our mission is threatened already—by violence!'

'That's hardly a promising start, is it?' replied the Doctor pleasantly. 'What has happened, exactly?'

On the balcony, all was ready. Grun had inserted the metal bar beneath the base of the statue. His hands rested on it lightly, ready to lever it from its base. He listened intently to the distant sound of voices coming from the throne room. Soon the audience would be ended and the aliens would enter the trap.

'The king's Chancellor has been killed!' squeaked Alpha Centauri.

'Destroyed by a legend,' observed Izlyr with chilly disbelief.

'It is a blatant attempt to intimidate the members of the Committee!' grated Arcturus.

The Doctor's voice cut across the babble of accusation like a schoolmaster correcting unruly infants.

'Gentlemen! We are members of a formal committee and not a gang of squabbling children!'

The group fell silent. It was Izlyr who spoke next.

'Your reproof is deserved, Chairman delegate. This discussion should be continued elsewhere.'

'Then let us proceed to the delegates' conference room,' rasped Arcturus.

'A splendid idea,' said the Doctor, and at Peladon's nod of agreement bowed and led the other delegates towards the throne room doors and out.

Grun heard the sound of the great doors being opened by the guard below. He took firm hold of the lever and set his full weight to it. First, it must reach the point of balance. After that, it would fall easily. His eyes watched for the telltale gap at the base of the statue. The sound of the aliens' movements below urged him to even greater efforts, and he felt the movement begin. One last thrust —and Aggedor would have his revenge!

45

## 4

## The Doctor Must Die

Outside the throne room, the Doctor paused and turned back to let Jo join him at the head of the group. He smiled politely at Izlyr who was standing close behind him, and started to speak—but the sentence never came. A fine drift of stone dust had fallen onto his cloak and, brushing it off, the Doctor looked upwards. Almost in the same movement, with a speed of reflex that would have done credit to a wild animal, he hurled himself at the group behind him, bringing them down all of a heap. They had not even reached the floor when the great stone image smashed into the ground beside them with a terrifying impact.

Peladon jumped to his feet and moved forward in alarm. Before he could reach the door, Hepesh had checked him, his face full of foreboding.

'No, majesty—there is danger! Wait!'

'But what has happened?' cried the young king, full of apprehension. 'If any of the delegates have been harmed ...' The rest of the sentence went unspoken, but the meaning was known to both the king and to Hepesh. The aliens had weapons not yet seen in action on Peladon. Their vengeance would surely be a terrible one.

'It is your majesty's safety that matters,' said Hepesh. But his eyes were not on the king. He was deliberately screening the return of Grun. Like a shadow, the King's Champion glided to his royal master's side. The king looked back at him, unaware that he had ever been away. But, thought Hepesh grimly, how well had he succeeded?

The Doctor, helping Jo to her feet, turned to find Izlyr standing over him, hand extended.

'You saved our lives, Doctor.' His harsh, hissing voice sounded genuinely grateful, but the Doctor could read nothing from his mask-like face.

'Sorry I didn't have time to explain,' joked the Doctor, and moved across to the shattered statue, its terrifying face turned upwards to the smoky ceiling. The guards nearby made no move to help. They crouched, heads bowed, moaning with fear.

'This is outrageous,' wailed Alpha Centauri, tentacles thrashing about wildly. 'Terrible! We could have been killed.' The hexapod's colour was palpitating green and blue.

Arcturus was, as expected, unemotional. He trundled close to the fallen statue.

'The gravitational forces involved were in excess of humanoid resistance,' he computed flatly. 'Serious damage would have resulted on impact.'

'Your objective reaction is admirable,' observed the Doctor drily, 'but you might've been killed too, Arcturus.'

'My sensor readings are not concerned with emotional response,' commented the mechanical voice, '—only deduction.'

'Even deductive processes can be annihilated,' said Izlyr, with icy reasoning.

'Alright, Jo?' asked the Doctor, seeing his young companion's drawn face grow even paler.

'Just a bit wobbly at the knees, that's all,' replied Jo bravely. She suddenly found herself pushed aside by Hepesh, who stood staring down at the shattered stone image.

'Aggedor has been merciful,' he spoke bleakly, silently registering the fact that, thanks to this new Earthling delegate, not one of the aliens had been harmed. He didn't allow his disappointment to show, however, as he raised his eyes to the Doctor's. 'We must give thanks that you have all been spared . . .'

'First Torbis dies,' observed Izlyr coldly. 'Now this.'

'Yes,' agreed the Doctor, 'but why didn't the Aggedor manifestation actually appear? Strange, that.'

'An investigation into the cause is necessary,' rasped Arcturus. 'A full report must be prepared!'

'The cause is simple,' exclaimed Hepesh. 'This is yet

47

another sign of Aggedor's anger! His ghost walks among us!'

'A pretty substantial ghost, then,' remarked the Doctor, looking up at the balcony above them, 'to be able to shift a solid granite statue.'

'The spirit of Aggedor can move mountains!' claimed the High Priest.

His face showed deep irritation at the alien's lack of piety and respect.

Jo had moved to a position where she could work out the trajectory of the statue from the balcony. 'It seems more like he was trying to remove *us*!'

Alpha Centauri had calmed down considerably, but was still distraught, its skin colour fluctuating wildly from mauve to pale green. 'But why should he seek to attack us?' the hexapod squealed. 'Our mission is peaceful. We come to raise the people of Peladon from barbarism!'

'Maybe they don't want to be raised,' muttered Jo, still staring at the layout of the balcony. The Doctor caught her eye, and nodded, indicating with a slight movement of his head where he thought access to the balcony could be found: close by the throne room doorway. As the others continued to query Hepesh's gloomy predictions of doom, Jo sidled quietly towards the doorway, unobserved.

'Hepesh,' demanded Izlyr impatiently, 'you say this manifestation is foretold in your ancient writings. What form is it supposed to take? Tell us that!'

'It is written,' declaimed the High Priest dramatically, 'that his coming shall be full of terror and darkness. His cry of warning shall be heard in the night, and death shall ride in the land of Peladon!'

Apart from Alpha Centauri, who trembled and turned a peculiar shade of green, the others were unimpressed, even sceptical.

'But there was no cry of warning,' pointed out the Doctor, 'and none of us saw him. You can't seriously count the statue as a spiritual appearance, can you?'

Hepesh glared at the Doctor through angry, narrowed

eyes, and snarled his reply. 'To the unbeliever, all signs are as dust upon the wind !'

'The point is,' said the Doctor, 'what does King Peladon believe?'

'If this religious administrator is the mouthpiece for the king's opinions,' hissed Izlyr, 'then our purpose here is wasted.'

Arcturus was quick to recognise the logic of this observation. 'If that is so, the conference must be cancelled,' the mechanical voice pronounced emphatically.

Hepesh tried not to show his feeling of triumph. His face remained impassive as he spoke with quiet dignity.

'That is the only answer,' he said. 'Any other course will surely mean disaster. Leave this planet while there is still time !'

'No!' Peladon cried out interrupting him. 'Do not listen to that old man ! Neither he nor Aggedor is king here. I am !'

'Majesty, there is no need,' offered Hepesh. But he was given no chance to continue.

'Be silent, Hepesh !' The young king gestured the alien delegates to return. 'Delegates, I ask you to rejoin me. Listen to what I have to say. Negotiations *must* go on !'

At this bold speech, the delegates turned their attention to the Doctor. As Chairman, the decision was his. The Doctor sensed the awful isolation of the young king as he fought so desperately for the future of his planet. Peladon must be given a chance, thought the Doctor, and stepped back towards him.

'I am prepared to listen to the king,' he said to the others, 'and perhaps you'd care to join us?'

Hepesh suddenly found himself left alone outside the throne room, and hurriedly followed the aliens inside. As he and the delegates took up their positions, the Doctor caught a brief glimpse of Jo's cloak as she slipped into the entry leading up to the balcony. No one else had noticed her departure. Everyone was listening to Izlyr as he addressed the king.

'Your majesty,' said the Martian warlord in that

strange whisper of a voice, 'negotiations are only possible in a peaceful situation.'

A clipped, factual observation followed quickly from Arcturus. 'Political conflict violates Federation law.'

'Centuries ago,' pleaded Peladon, 'on your own planets, war and violence flourished!'

Alpha Centauri, almost back to normal at last, piped, 'We have learned to control our past.'

'Then teach Peladon!' cried the young king. 'How can we raise ourselves from the Dark Ages without help? Do not desert us now!'

Outside the closed throne room doors, the guards were clearing away the rubble of the smashed statue. As Jo came to the top of the tightly twisting stairway that led onto the balcony, she realised that to go any further would be to risk discovery. She paused, and crouched. It was all too obvious what had been done. There was the metal bar and the stone that had acted as fulcrum to the lever. More important, set into the dust of the rarely used balcony was one mighty footprint. Huge, bigger than any footprint she had seen, in Jo's mind it could belong to only one person: Ssorg, the Ice Warrior. She thought of his size, and strength. She couldn't remember if he had been present in the throne room all the time, but if she had managed to slip away unnoticed, why couldn't he? But she remembered that Izlyr had been close behind the Doctor when the statue fell. If Ssorg was responsible, why had he endangered his chief? Was he in fact in league with someone else? Or was she just imagining things—building up a ridiculous case on the basis of one smudged footprint? A movement from below startled her from her train of thought, and she drew back into the shadows. As she did so, a glint of light caught a small metallic object, half-hidden by the block of stone used as a fulcrum. From where she stood, Jo couldn't see it clearly. She realised that it would mean moving out into the open before she could pick it up. She peered anxiously down past the edge of the stone platform, trying to see the position of the guards. Unless she moved quickly, she would be missed from the group inside the throne room. And if she was discovered up here, how would she talk her way out of that? For a moment, the guards turned away, quietly talking. With a quick, supple movement, Jo leaned forward on her hands and knees, grasped the piece of shining metal, and retreated back into the safety of the shadows. She didn't wait to inspect what she had found. It was time to return to the Doctor.

The Committee were still considering Peladon's plea that they should remain, when Jo arrived at the bottom of the concealed staircase. She paused in the shadow there, before moving forward quietly. No one seemed to have noticed her absense, or her return. She positioned herself to catch the Doctor's eye. He nodded, imperceptibly, pleased that she was safely back. Izlyr was speaking.

'If we remain,' he whispered deliberately, 'we put ourselves at risk!'

'But we *are* free to go,' twittered Alpha Centauri. 'Is that not so, King Peladon?'

'Do you seriously believe that I would keep you here by force?' replied the young ruler.

'Such things have been known to occur on other primitive planets,' observed the nervous hexapod. 'We cannot rule out such a possibility!'

'But why should I detain you?' asked the king, his face reflecting his obvious surprise.

'As pawns in some political game . . .' clipped Arcturus. 'But to do so would be most unwise!'

Peladon almost laughed, but his face quickly became serious. 'There is no plot against you. Please stay. Help me . . . and help my people!'

The Doctor glanced at the others, then spoke quietly to the king.

'We will adjourn and consider what you have said, your majesty,' remarked the Doctor, sympathetically. 'You'll know our decision as soon as possible.'

The king nodded, and with a motion of his hand, ended the audience. The aliens turned and moved after the Doctor towards the throne room doors, with Jo joining the edge of the departing group. But the king's voice stopped her. He stepped down from his throne and moved towards her, hand outstretched.

'Princess Jo, would you remain, please?' he said.

Jo looked over her shoulder, hoping for guidance from the Doctor, but he was almost outside now, and deep in conversation with Alpha Centauri. She looked back at the king. There was only friendliness in his face—and it would be nice to talk to someone of her own age . . . and human, for once.

'Of course, your majesty,' she murmured, and moved to the stool he indicated. As she sat, Peladon turned to the only other persons in the room—Grun, and Hepesh. Grun's weathered features were expressionless, but Hepesh was obviously displeased at the young king's informal manner with this Earthling maiden. Peladon gave him no chance to object.

'Grun, Hepesh, you may leave.'

The look in Peladon's eye made Hepesh realise it would be better to leave without comment. With Grun, he bowed and departed. As the young man who ruled Peladon moved back to his throne, Jo's mind raced. What on earth do you talk about, to a king?'

For a moment neither of them spoke. It was Peladon who at last broke the silence, His eyes studied Jo intently.

'Do *you* believe me?' he asked bluntly.

'I'm only an observer,' Jo answered, flustered by his directness. 'It's up to the Committee to decide whether to help you or not.'

Peladon smiled. 'I'm speaking from a personal point of view. I don't often get the chance.'

'I'd've thought that being a king was fun!' replied Jo brightly. 'Think of all the things you can do!'

A sad smile moved Peladon's mouth, and he shook his head before replying, 'It's not just a vocation or a lifetime's task that I'm trained to do. It's very lonely.' He paused, then reminded her that she too was supposedly of royal descent. 'You must know that.'

Jo knew what he meant, but couldn't deny the lie. 'Oh,

yes . . . I do know,' she said sympathetically. 'But what about Hepesh? He seems very close to you, almost like a father.'

'Hepesh is like your friend, the Doctor,' replied Peladon with a dry smile, 'an old man.'

Jo laughed. 'I don't suppose either of them would much like to hear you say that.'

'My whole life has been guided by wise old men,' reflected the young king. 'I hardly ever meet anyone of my own age,' his face grew sombre, 'now that my mother is dead. She was an Earthwoman, too. So you see, there is a bond between us . . .'

It wasn't difficult for Jo to feel sympathy for the young king. In the past, she too had known what it was to be alone and friendless, and she could understand the hope in his face as he moved towards her and took her hand.

'*Do* you believe me?' he asked.

Jo faced him without flinching, and nodded. 'Yes,' she said, 'I think I do. But I don't see how I can help.'

Her offer was sincere and honest; but when Peladon replied, Jo felt a wave of disappointment sweep over her.

'You can speak on my behalf to the Commission. Make them see my case!'

'I see,' said Jo, pulling away in alarm. 'It's a political ally you want; someone to pull a few strings, on the sly!'

Peladon's face showed his dismay at Jo's rejection. He thought he had won her over, but now . . . 'I'm telling the truth,' he said. 'I want you as a friend!'

'Sorry,' insisted Jo, coolly, 'I'm strictly neutral. You can count me out.'

Without another word, she turned and left. Peladon could only watch her go, his face frowning with disappointment.

.    .    .    .    .

The Temple of Aggedor, like the holy statues of the Royal Beast, was immense and oppressive in its majesty. The huge stone representation of the Royal Beast gave it an atmosphere of the supernatural. Streams of smoking incense rose from the plain altar. A ritual musical instrument wailed in the gloom. The flickering lights of the wall torches, filtered and weirdly distorted by the incense smoke, made the great statue eerie with dark shadows, and rising above the soft vibration of the distant music came the penetrating voice of the High Priest, intoning an ancient incantation. His plea—spoken in the ritual tongue—rose up to the impassive, terrifying mask of the Royal Beast; and when at last he fell silent, he turned about and faced the only other person in the temple : the muscular form of Grun, prostrate and grovelling before Hepesh's feet.

'You are forgiven, Grun,' intoned the priest. 'The failure was not yours. You acted with true belief, but Aggedor was merciful to his enemies !'

With a light touch of his bejewelled hand, Hepesh tilted Grun's awestruck face upwards and gazed deeply into his troubled eyes. His face grew cruel as he spoke.

'But the hour of mercy has passed, Grun! The aliens have had their chance, and they have refused !'

Grun looked into the eyes of his High Priest, and saw the anger there, mingling with the power that only Aggedor ordained. He knew he was about to be commanded to a new and urgent task, and, wonderingly, waited. His will became lost in the darkness of Hepesh's eyes, and the voice that came to him through Hepesh's mouth was like that of Aggedor himself.

'Grun, an evil influence has come between our king and his true destiny. It must be destroyed and, to this end, Aggedor gives his blessing.'

Overawed by the purpose that was to be his destiny, Grun bowed his head beneath the poised hands of the High Priest, who now intoned the evil blessing.

'You, Grun, are the King's Champion. I dedicate you to the destruction of the king's enemies : to purify the soul of Peladon by this act of vengeance and give the ghost of Aggedor release.' The ringed hands made a strange sign over Grun's bowed head, and then the voice

54

'*You are forgiven, Grun.*'

continued, more harshly. 'The task is set. Now know that the foremost of the king's enemies is the Chairman delegate from Earth, the one they call the Doctor.'

Grun looked up questioningly at the face of the High Priest.

'Destroy him, Grun,' commanded Hepesh.

5

## The Attack on Arcturus

The Doctor was examining the small metal object which Jo had found on the balcony over the throne room door. She had decided not to tell him about King Peladon's request. At last he gave a small grunt of recognition, and Jo leaned forward eagerly.

'Well, what is it?'

'Its an electronic key, Jo,' murmured the Doctor, passing her the eyeglass and the object. The Doctor smiled.

'It opens doors by identifying the bearer electronically,' he explained. 'Probably used for their spaceship, I shouldn't wonder.'

'Used for *whose* spaceship?' demanded Jo.

'Why, the Ice Warriors, of course.' The Doctor took the key back from her, and tucked his eyeglass into an already bulging pocket. 'It's made from trisilicate. Remarkable stuff, found only on Mars.'

'Then that footprint I found—' said Jo eagerly, '—do you think it *was* made by Ssorg?'

'Highly likely, I'd say, Jo,' mused the Doctor.

'That's what I thought, when I saw the mark in the dust,' agreed Jo. 'But I'm almost certain he was with us in the throne room all the time.'

'You slipped away without anyone noticing, remember.'

Jo had to admit that this was true. But that still didn't explain the reason for what Ssorg had done.

'But he nearly killed Izlyr as well!' she pointed out. 'And even if that was just some sort of cover up, what would they be after here?'

The Doctor nodded thoughtfully. Jo could be right about the cover-up. As for what the Ice Warriors might be after . . .

'When I knew them before, Jo, they wanted to colonise Earth. And you may have noticed that this planet, backward though it is, is very much like ours.'

Jo wasn't at all sure that the Doctor was right. 'But they're here for the same reason as the other delegates—peace,' she said.

'Are they, Jo? I know them, remember. I've seen what they're capable of doing. Not only are they technically highly advanced, but they're also a ruthless and warlike race. I'm afraid I don't trust them.'

'And you're always telling *me* to look for the good qualities in alien life forms!'

'The Ice Warriors are the exception to that rule, Jo. For me, at any rate. I'm telling you, I've met them twice so far, and they only have one aim—conquest!'

'I still think you could be jumping to conclusions,' Jo retorted.

'Alright then, look at it another way. Who else could be responsible? Arcturus is only a box of tricks. *He* certainly couldn't've got up to that balcony!'

Jo nodded in agreement. She didn't especially like Arcturus, but he was hardly an athlete.

'And as for Alpha Centauri,' continued the Doctor, 'I can't imagine a creature like that harming a fly, can you? But whether it's the Ice Warriors or not . . . I wish I knew just what it is they're up to.'

The familiar expression that Jo was getting to know so well crept over the Doctor's face. He'd caught a whiff of adventure. More than that, he wouldn't be satisfied until he'd got to the bottom of it—unless Jo put her foot down.

'Look, Doctor,' she insisted firmly, 'do we have to find out? Why don't we just organise getting the TARDIS dug out, and get out of here? You know what happens when

57

you get involved. Look what happened in the throne room!'

'I didn't really have any choice, Jo,' the Doctor protested defensively.

'Oh, come on! You love all that Chairman Delegate stuff. Admit it!

Jo had scored a bullseye. Without bothering to deny what she had said, the Doctor merely looked at her with a wicked twinkle in his eye.

'And how do *you* like being a princess, Princess?'

Jo blushed, but her chin tilted defiantly.

'As you said yourself, there wasn't much choice, was there?' Suddenly, she whirled round. She could hear a strange, high-pitched sound, pulsing sharply. The eerie tone was definitely electronic, and Jo's eyes widened in alarm. 'What's that?' she cried, clutching the Doctor's arm.

'It's an alarm of some sort!' he exclaimed, already moving towards the door. 'And it's coming from the delegates' conference room! Quickly!'

As soon as the Doctor entered the delegates' room, he could see what was wrong. Apart from the shrill audio signal that Arcturus was giving out so desperately, various telemetric warnings lights were flashing on and off about the globe that contained the Arcturian neuroform. Crouching by the complex traction and support unit, the Doctor soon found the cause. A whole series of plugs and wiring had been exposed and torn out. As he studied the tangle that was destroying Arcturus, Jo came to his shoulder, and looked down. She gasped in horror at the sight of the disembowelled life-support unit.

'Doctor, what can you do?' she whispered, not needing to ask how great the danger was. It showed in the violent discoloration of the neuroplasm, and the almost complete misting over of the interior of the containing globe. Unless something was done quickly, Arcturus would die.

The Doctor was searching desperately amongst the tangle of electronic circuitry. He mumbled to himself as he identified the various strands. Then he suddenly sat back and looked about the floor, sharp-eyed.

'Someone's taken the servo-function unit, Jo—' he snapped. 'There's no time to waste looking for it. I'll have to bypass the junction and relink the circuits manually!'

Jo realised she could do nothing to help. The insistent ping of the Arcturian alarm system was giving her a headache. She left the Doctor to his own devices while she tried to locate the missing electronic gadget.

'Doctor, what does this servo thing look like?'

'Sort of . . . transparent . . . cube,' muttered the Doctor, engrossed in his work, 'lots of . . . fine circuitry inside.'

Jo was puzzled. 'It couldn't just've fallen out of Arcturus,' she said. 'And I can't see it anywhere.'

'Quite right, Jo,' mumbled the Doctor. 'This wasn't an accident. You see—'

Jo's eyes widened. 'Someone tried to kill him?'

'Tried,' nodded the Doctor, then frowned and continued working, frantically, 'and they may yet succeed— unless I'm successful first!'

The shrill alarm signal was now only intermittent, and the transparent globe clouded completely. The life process would surely reach critical soon.

'If his metabolism subsides into a catatonic state, there'll be no hope at all . . .' gritted the Doctor. His fingers were working with incredible speed, and the intensity on his face was almost frightening.

'So whoever removed that servo-function cube tried to kill Arcturus—and may have been responsible for all the other so-called accidents as well!' Jo thought aloud.

'Quite the Sherlock Holmes, aren't you, Jo,' mumbled the Doctor.

'So if we could find the cube . . .'

'No, Jo. That could prove far too dangerous. Just leave things to me, there's a good girl.'

Jo didn't give up easily. 'I could search the delegates rooms. I might just find something,' she insisted. 'Then we'd have some real evidence. It'd make all the difference.'

The Doctor didn't answer. He was far too involved in beating the clock. It was Jo who saw Izlyr stride into the room and stand over Arcturus. The alarm was now so feeble as to be non-existent.

'What are you doing to Arcturus?' demanded the warlord.

The Doctor looked up at the Martian looming over him, but didn't stop what he was doing.

'Someone has disconnected and removed a vital part of his life-support system. I'm trying to save him. Go away there's a good chap!'

For a moment, Izlyr seemed uncertain what to do, and his deep hissing breathing was the only easily heard sound in the room. Suddenly, the Doctor, extricated himself from the debris on the floor, beamed at Izlyr and Jo, and started tucking odds and ends of equipment back inside Arcturus.

'There, old chap,' said the Doctor, patting the globe gently. 'That should do the trick.'

'Have you succeeded?' demanded Izlyr harshly.

'He'll be alright in a little while, I think,' responded the Doctor. 'A bit of a near thing, though.'

As the Doctor clambered to his feet, Alpha Centauri and Hepesh appeared in the doorway. They moved forward to see what had caused the alarm. With the doorway clear, Jo took her chance. If the Doctor's earlier suspicions were right, she knew exactly where she would find the missing electronic cube.

'Another attack on Federation personnel?' trilled Alpha Centauri in alarm. 'This is dreadful!'

'This was the work of Aggedor,' said Hepesh in a voice of doom.

'Absolute nonsense,' cheerfully observed the Doctor. 'This was the work of a skilled technician, and your medieval monster, Hepesh, is hardly that. He'd simply try to smash Arcturus' protective globe.'

'You are not surely suggesting,' squeaked the hexapod, turning a rich shade of purple, 'that we of the Federation are to blame?'

'If that is an accusation,' hissed Izlyr fiercely, 'I deny it!'

The Doctor ignored Hepesh and Alpha Centauri, and confronted Izlyr boldly. 'Of course you'd deny it, Izlyr. But you *do* have the necessary technical know-how. Do you deny that?'

'The technology of Alpha Centauri is also competent enough!' exclaimed the warlord. 'So is that of Earth. And it was you, Doctor, that we found tampering with our colleague's life-support system!'

'Then it's thanks to me that he'll be able to identify his attacker,' retorted the Doctor. 'And that should be very shortly.'

. . . . . .

The room that Jo entered was, like all those allocated to the alien delegates, a stark, stone chamber made elegant by rich furniture and wall hangings—but basically primitive for all that. The door had been closed, but unlocked. No one had answered Jo's discreet knock, and when eventually she plucked up enough nerve to enter, the room was deserted. Closing the door quietly behind her, she stood against it and surveyed the room. The mere presence of the Ice Warriors seemed to have turned the place into a barrack room. Items of military equipment were laid out neatly everywhere, as though ready for inspection. An important feature was what looked like a communications set, but there was no sign of life from it. Jo moved about the room quickly and silently, looking for the telltale electronic cube that would confirm the Doctor's suspicions. She could find nothing remotely like it. Finally, she came to a compact box that seemed to be made of the same material as the electronic key she had found earlier on the balcony. It had no lock, and opened easily. But Jo, being human, couldn't hear the sonic frequency the box emitted as its security system. She only had eyes for the contents inside : several elaborate tools—and the servolink cube! The Doctor had been right!

Jo picked up the transparent cube with trembling fingers and held it up to the light. Inside was an intricate maze of embedded filaments, the circuitry that, once removed, could destroy Arcturus. She frowned. Why should the Ice Warriors try to kill anyone in such a complicated way? She had seen the wrist-gun on Ssorg's arm, and its deadly efficiency had been fully described by the Doctor. Suddenly, a sound from outside the door startled her. As the handle started to turn, she concealed herself behind one of the ornate tapestries. The material was so dusty that it was all she could do not to sneeze or cough. Hidden behind the thick folds, she could see nothing, and her imagination magnified the least sound. The heavy shuffling movements were unmistakable: Ssorg, the Ice Warrior, had entered the room. Jo held her breath. Although she had replaced everything else precisely as she had found it, she had made one mistake: the box in which she had found the cube was still open! The sound of his feet stopped. All she could hear was the serpent-like hiss of his breathing. Then, he was moving again. But where? Jo quickly found out. A mighty hand tore the tapestry aside and she found herself face to face with the grim warrior. She couldn't even scream.

'Earth Princess,' Ssorg whispered accusingly, 'why are you here?'

Jo gripped the transparent cube defiantly. 'I was looking for something—and I found it!'

The huge Martian made no attempt to snatch her discovery from her. Instead, he inspected it very carefully—almost as though seeing it for the first time.

'This object,' he hissed, slowly pondering, 'it does not belong here. It is not ours.'

'I know it isn't!' exclaimed Jo. 'It belongs to Arcturus! You tried to kill him!'

The Martian stared at Jo, but still made no threatening move. Out of the corner of her eye, Jo saw that the door was open. Could she make a dash for it?

'You are the intruder here,' breathed Ssorg harshly. 'You have opened equipment that is not yours to touch. I heard the sonic warning, and I came.'

'That's where I found this servo-link!' snapped Jo angrily. 'Only you didn't hide it very cleverly, did you?'

It was the Ice Warrior's turn to be angry. 'You say you found this. I say you were putting it where it would later be found to incriminate my master, Izlyr!'

'That's a lie!' cried Jo in desperate protest, and tried to escape—but too late. Ssorg's mighty fist gripped her by the wrist. With his other huge hand, he took the transparent cube from her with surprising care. Jo was completely helpless in his grasp. Ssorg pushed her roughly into a nearby chair. She stared up at him, in terror.

'You will stay here,' declared the Martian. 'I must inform Lord Izlyr of what has happened.'

Then, taking the cube, he strode out, closing the heavy wooden door after him. Jo ran to the door, but trying to open it was hopeless. As she reached it, she could hear the sound of heavy bolts being rammed home. She leaned her face against the wood in despair. She was trapped.

．　　　．　　　．　　　．　　　．

It was clear from the upward peaking of his Metabolism Pulse Modulator that Arcturus was rapidly recovering; but until he was in a fit state to speak, the delegates clustered about him, tense with anticipation. In the background, Hepesh glowered grimly, but his comments largely went unheeded. What Arcturus had to say was far more important.

'Why do you not believe me?' demanded the High Priest. 'Aggedor has shown that he can use your own technology to defeat and even destroy you! Leave our world while you still can!'

'Not before we've found what's behind all this, Hepesh,' murmured the Doctor, watching the globe that contained the Arcturian neuroform. It was virtually clear now. 'It's rather important to us all, I'd say.'

'Let us hope there is no permanent neural damage,' hissed Izlyr. 'Arcturus,' asked the Martian, as the tendrils of the neuroform began to move gently, 'can you hear me? Do you know what has happened?'

Hepesh moved closer, keen-faced, as everyone waited for Arcturus' answer. It came only with great hesitation.

63

'I . . . have been . . . attacked . . .' rasped the slurre metallic voice. 'Attacked . . .'

'Who was it?' shrilled Alpha Centauri excitedly. 'Di you see who?'

'Speak, Arcturus!' commanded Izlyr. 'We must know

'Was the face of Aggedor revealed to you, alien?' crie Hepesh.

'Give him a chance,' muttered the Doctor. 'He's sti suffering from shock, poor chap.'

Arcturus' voicebox cleared its throat electronically 'Memory circuits . . . out of phase . . . something violen . . . happened to me . . . but . . . I do not . . . remembe . . .' The halting voice finally broke down. It was obviousl not going to be easy.

'A dreadful experience,' piped Alpha Centauri in sym pathy.

'Looks as if we'll have to ask him later,' mused th Doctor, frowning. He moved away. 'Pity, that.'

'We cannot wait!' insisted Izlyr. 'The matter is too im portant! We must know now!'

'Cannot . . . remember . . .' repeated Arcturus pitiably 'Cannot remember . . .'

The computerised tones faded to an electronic hum as Arcturus endeavoured to pull himself together. Izly turned. The Doctor was strolling thoughtfully toward the door. Izlyr called out to him sharply.

'Doctor, where are you going?'

'Don't worry, Izlyr, I'm not fleeing the country,' replie the Doctor. 'Just studying the lie of the land, that's all His last words came from the corridor outside.

Izlyr made no attempt to stop him, but was not satis fied. He turned back to the passive neuroplasm, deter mined that it should speak—and name its attacker.

.    .    .    .    .    .

No point in trying to pick the lock with a hairpin, J thought. That crafty Martian has bolted it. It looked a though she'd be forced to sit and wait until Ssorg re

64

turned with his boss, Izlyr—and then the fun would start.
If it came to her word against Ssorg, it was obvious which
would count most. And then not only Jo but the Doctor
himself would be in dead trouble. She sighed, despondently. All because that blessed box had been connected
to some sort of warning system! The Doctor was right—
they knew what they were up to, these Martians! The
more Jo thought about that, the more she wanted to wake
up and find that everything so far was just a bad dream.
She pinched herself. It hurt. She sat down wearily, ready
to resign herself to what was to follow. It was like being
in the condemned cell. She looked about her, morosely—
then looked again. High up on the far wall, there was a
window, open and unbarred. She still had a chance.

Beneath the window opening, there were sockets in
the wall. Timbers had been there once, and Jo guessed it
had probably been an archer's window. The platform
they had once stood upon to fire their arrows at the
enemy was gone now. If Jo could get up there she was sure
she'd be slim enough to slip through! Anyway, it was
better than nothing. The question was: how to reach the
window ledge. The table she pushed to the wall beneath
the window was nowhere near high enough. A sturdy
chair on top of the table was better, but still not right.
Then her eye fell on the box where she'd found the servo-
unit. It was closed now, and it would give her that extra
bit of height. But dared she use it? Would it give her away
again? She looked around quickly and saw that nothing
else would do. Placing the box on top of the chair, Jo
began to climb.

It wasn't easy, and more than once she nearly toppled
and fell. Finally, she managed to scramble on to the window ledge. She found it surprisingly broad—from below it
had seemed much smaller. And the window itself was
wide enough for her to squeeze through. It wasn't until
she saw just how high up she was, and that her escape
would entail edging along a foot-wide band of stone on the
wall outside, that Jo began to have second thoughts. The
wind had subsided, but the distance to the courtyard far

below seemed immense. Her plan was to creep along unt
she came to a window opening into another room, an
then find her way back to the Doctor. Taking a dee
breath, she wriggled outside. The cold night air made he
gasp. Then, flattened hard back against the wall of th
citadel, poised high above the stone courtyard, Jo bega
to inch along to her left. Her eyes closed tight to prever
even the briefest glance below, and her hands spread wid
feeling for the opening she needed, she had a sudde
flicker of memory: the Doctor, telling her to let him d
things his way. Well, he wasn't around to help her now

    •    •    •    •    •

Deep in thought, the Doctor was hardly aware of hi
surroundings as he paced along the castle corridor. Hi
total concentration on the problem of who was wher
when the incident that nearly killed Arcturus happenec
had made him forget the possible dangers of the shadow
passage. But when a huge fist gripped him by the shoulde
and turned him from his path, he was instantly alert, han
raised to defend himself with the famous Venusian 'loxka
—the straight-fingered jab at the carotid throat arter
that could, if necessary, prove fatal. The face before hir
showed surprise at his speed of movement. Recognisin
the muscular figure of the King's Champion, the Docto
checked the blow, inches from its target.

'You really shouldn't creep up on a chap like tha
Grun,' the Doctor reproved mildly. 'What d'you want?

The mute warrior could only grunt. But his mime
gesture was clear enough for the Doctor to understand.

'You want me to go with you, is that it?' translate
the Doctor as Grun beckoned him, nodding to indicat
that the Doctor had interpreted correctly. 'But why?'

With deft movements of hands and fingers, Grun indi
cated Jo's long hair and height. For a moment, the Docto
looked mystified. Then realising, he frowned.

'You mean Jo—the princess? Is something wrong?'

Grun nodded vigorously, but his face was serious. H

eckoned again, more urgently, and started to move away.
'Then she's in trouble?'

Grun's hand pulled at the Doctor's arm, and now the
Doctor didn't resist, but urged the burly warrior to lead
n.

'Alright, old chap, I get the message. But where are we
oing?'

Grun paused to indicate a shadowy passage leading
rom the main corridor. Convinced by his emphatic ges-
ure, the Doctor nodded and followed the King's Cham-
ion into the darkness beyond. He did not see the figure
n the shadows that watched him go. It was Hepesh the
High Priest. And he was smiling . . .

# 6

# The Temple of Aggedor

Arcturus, although recovered and fully functional, could
ill not remember clearly what had happened to him.
zlyr, however, was growing increasingly suspicious of the
Doctor.

'I saw no one, delegate Ixlyr,' clipped Arcturus. 'The
ttack was too sudden.'

'The Doctor claimed to be saving your life,' insisted
he warlord, 'but he could just as easily have been destroy-
ng your life-support system.'

Alpha Centauri was less convinced. 'But what motive
ould he possibly have?'

'Ask his masters on Earth!' retorted Izlyr. 'They are
evious men!'

'And why has he brought this princess?' rapped out
rcturus. 'She has no official standing!'

'A diplomatic courtesy, surely,' suggested Alpha
Centauri. 'After all, Peladon's mother was an Earthling.'

'And if Peladon was to marry this Earth princess?'

Izlyr's words produced a thoughtful silence. 'The inte
blood alliance would be strengthened to Earth's advan
tage within the Federation. It would be *their* thinkin
that would guide Peladon's rulers.'

'That must not be allowed to happen!' rasped Ar
turus.

Just as Alpha Centauri was about to intercede, all ey
looked to the door. Ssorg had entered.

'Lord Izlyr,' he whispered urgently, 'I must speak wit
you.'

Izlyr excused himself and moved to Ssorg. Arcturu
confided in Alpha Centauri, who was rapidly becomin
anxious once again.

'What is happening?' the hexapod asked.

'There has obviously been a new development,' replie
Arcturus, adding maliciously, 'I doubt if it will be ben
ficial to our mission.'

'Oh,' sighed Alpha Centauri despondently, 'what
barbarous planet this is!'

Izlyr returned to his colleagues, with Ssorg at his sid
At his silent command, Ssorg presented his find to th
other delegates. There followed an ominous silence.

'The missing servo-link has been found by sub-delega
Ssorg,' whispered Izlyr, indicating the precious objec

'Where was it?' demanded Arcturus sharply.

'In the hands of the Earthling princess. Alpha Centaur
perhaps you will assist our friend Arcturus by replacing it

'Of course,' trilled Alpha Centauri, and quickly s
about the task.

'But why should the Earth princess wish to harm me
grated Arcturus. Izlyr paused at the doorway.

'That is what I intend to find out,' hissed the warlor
'Come, Ssorg.' And, together, the two Martians move
purposefully towards the room where Jo had been le
prisoner.

. . ∎ . .

At last Jo's hand felt the welcome shape of the windo
edge. Relieved, she lowered herself down and through th

narrow opening. For a moment she sat, quite still, on the interior window ledge, and looked about her. It wasn't a room, but a section of corridor. Gloomy and poorly lit by flickering torches, it made her shiver! But she had escaped from the Ice Warriors! Jo lowered herself gingerly, then dropped the remaining distance and landed lightly on her toes. She looked about her, and knew she was lost. She frowned, not frightened, but thinking hard. First, she had to get to the Doctor, and tell him what had happened. Secondly, she had to make sure she avoided Izlyr and Ssorg. But which way was she to go? Keeping to the shadows, she moved along the corridor, and tried to get her bearings. It was useless. The only distinguishing feature about the various castle passages was the difference in the tapestries that hung here and there. All Jo could say for certain was that she hadn't seen any of these particular wall hangings before. But the corridor had to lead somewhere, she thought to herself desperately. She remembered how huge the citadel had seemed from outside, and groaned inwardly. She could probably walk for days and still be lost! Coming to a junction of three corridors, she paused. The darker, less well-lit ones offered more safety in their shadows. But the brighter one might lead her to safety! Jo set off down this corridor with a new spring in her step.

.     .     .     .     .

The Doctor watched Grun's broad back warily. He had followed the burly warrior for what seemed ages, doubling and twisting through the labyrinth of castle corridors until in the normal course of events, the Doctor would have been well and truly lost. Which was precisely what was intended, the Doctor decided. He chuckled to himself. Someone, somewhere must think he was a fool. He had carefully memorised the route by a simple method—the tapestries they had passed on their way. Each one had featured a different combination of designs, and the Doctor's remarkable memory had carefully stored these images in precisely the correct order. Grun might think he was being rather clever, and the Doctor wasn't going to disillusion him . . . yet. First, the Doctor wanted to see just where Grun was leading him. He was sure it wasn't to Jo. Pretending to be duped was taking a dangerous chance, he knew. But if it brought him closer to the power behind the threat to the delegates, it would be worth it. Suddenly, for no apparent reason, Grun stopped. The Doctor tensed, ready for trouble. Grun, however, merely pointed to a tapestry before them which was set in a dark alcove of the passage. With a quickening of his pulse, the Doctor recognised it. It was identical to the one he and Jo had seen when they had first entered the palace! Grun pulled the tapestry to one side. He gave a twist to the nearby torch holder. With a low groan of rarely used hinges, the wall slowly opened—but only wide enough for a man to squeeze through. Inside the secret tunnel which was now revealed, the Doctor saw the flicker of more torches. Grun mimed that the Doctor should go in.

'This way?' queried the Doctor pleasantly, alert to the slightest move that Grun might make to attack him. Grun nodded, motioning for the Doctor to go first. With a charming smile, the Doctor indicated that Grun should lead the way.

'Not at all, my dear chap, after you,' he said, miming his words to reinforce the point. Surprisingly, Grun made no further objection. He squeezed his muscular bulk into the tunnel beyond. With a slight frown, the Doctor followed. A second later, the wall panel closed, the tapestry fell back into place, and they had gone from sight. It was as though they had never been there at all . . .

.    .    .    .    .

Jo paused, telling herself not to panic. The corridor swept ahead in a great unending curve. Surely she would recognise something or someone soon! She shivered. For some reason, it grew suddenly cold. The torch flames flickered and leaned, as though a wind was passing over them, or a great door had been opened in the darkness beyond. Jo shrugged, took a step forward, then froze in terror. From somewhere along the corridor—impossible to tell yet whether from in front or behind her—came the deep throbbing howl she had heard when she and the Doctor had first entered the citadel! Alert, she stood uncertain which way to run. Then, when she saw the looming shape that came towards her from the corridor ahead, she screamed. As though in answer, that hideous cry rang out again. Into the full light of the wall torches stepped Aggedor.

The images and the carving that Jo had already seen were like picture postcards in comparison. The jet-black, silky hair that covered the monster, curled and twisted into bizarre shapes, seemed to add to its huge dimensions. From deep in the skull, two flashing, bloodshot eyes stared and glittered in bestial fury. Above the nostrils a ferocious white tusk gleamed. Two tusk-like fang teeth projected from the ferocious mouth. The great beast reared above her, seeming to fill the whole passageway. In one split second, Jo took in all this—and, turning, ran for her life!

Jo knew that her cloak would only hinder her escape. She let it fall to the ground behind her, and continued running. She began to sprint more rapidly to put a greater distance between herself and the beast and, turning a corner, cannoned into Ssorg! Held fast in his mighty arms she could do nothing but point to the corridor behind her. Izlyr, motioning for Ssorg to release her, questioned Jo sternly.

'You were a prisoner in our room. How did you escape?'

Gulping for air, Jo struggled to reply. 'Never mind . . . about that!' she gasped. 'The monster, Aggedor . . . He's coming this way!'

Izlyr's mask-like face showed no response, but his voice was full of mistrust.

'We shall see,' he said, and gestured for Ssorg to investigate, while in turn held Jo captive.

'But he'll be killed!' protested Jo feebly.

'Do not be afraid for Ssorg,' retorted the proud war-lord, 'his sonic weapon can destroy any living creature —if it actually exists!'

But Ssorg was only paces from them when, more distant now but just as menacing, came the fearsome cry of Aggedor, the Royal Beast, yet again.

.     .     .     .     .

At the first distant howl, Grun had faltered, but as it rang out again, closer and more terrible, he stopped altogether. Unable to see the warrior's rugged face in the half-darkness, the Doctor assumed that Grun was merely being careful. But when he came closer, and looked into the eyes of the King's Champion, he saw the deep terror.

'Grun,' asked the Doctor quietly, 'what is it?'

Grun looked at him and grunted his fear. Again, the sound rang out, nearer this time. With a bellow of dismay Grun broke away from the Doctor and ran. Within seconds, he was lost to sight in the gloomy shadows of an unlit side tunnel. The Doctor's voice echoed after him.

'Grun! Wait!'

It was no use. Grun had vanished. The Doctor was completely alone.

The Doctor stood quite still, carefully taking in his bearings and listening keenly for any further sounds of what must be Aggedor. This explanation fitted with what he had already been told about the death of Torbis. It would also account for Grun's desperate fear. Only a so-called ghostly being could terrify a man like Grun to that extent—and, perversely, made the Doctor all the more determined to see the apparition for himself. He wondered if this was the reason for Grun leading him to this secret place—to meet Aggedor and suffer the same dreadful fate as Torbis. But why, if Grun was leading the Doctor to Aggedor, did the warrior bolt in terror? Was there something yet more terrible in store which Grun had not foreseen? There was only one way to find out. His eyes glinting with determination, the Doctor moved forward. Aggedor permitting, he would know the answers very soon.

The tunnel had now become a shallow staircase, turning in a broad spiral higher and higher. The torches here, more ornate and worked in a rarer metal, were in better condition than those in the lower tunnels. The Doctor moved slowly forward, careful of ambush or a trap. If the Pels were anything like Earthlings of the fifteenth century, they'd be certain to think up something clever—and unpleasant! But the journey ended safely in a blank stone wall similar to the one previously encountered by the Doctor and Jo. Casually, he looked for and found the wall torch that controlled the secret door. It opened and he went through. Immediately, he knew that he had come to a very special place.

He had entered the inner sanctum of a temple dedicated to the Royal Beast. As the secret door closed after him, the Doctor took in the eerie majesty of the great statue, the acrid tang of the incense smoke, and the weird music of unseen instruments. For a long moment, he stood before the statue, admiring the workmanship and engineering of the massive replica. It was comparable to the huge statues of the Egyptian pharoahs. In the hazy light, it was difficult to see just what it was carved from. He moved closer to examine and touch. He had barely passed the simple stone altar, and laid his hand on the granite of the statue, when a sharp voice, distorted by the acoustics of the temple walls, rang out accusingly.

'Sacrilege! An unholy intruder!'

The Doctor spun about, and saw his accuser's jewelled finger pointing accusingly. It was Hepesh.

'Grun,' he shouted jubilantly, 'seize him!'

From a shadowed doorway on the far side of the altar, Grun strode forward, sword in hand. He had been waiting, realised the Doctor. This was the trap. He turned to Hepesh to explain but one glance at his face told the Doctor that he could expect no mercy there. The triumph in his voice told the Doctor more than the formal horror of his words. Hepesh had not merely sprung the trap;

he had planned it. The brain behind the curse of Aggedor was that of the High Priest, not an alien. But speculation was useless without proof; and the Doctor was Grun's prisoner.

The Doctor saw at a glance that Grun was in an induced trance. The sword in his hand was no ornament: any sign of resistance and it would be used, ruthlessly. The Doctor had no intention of presenting Hepesh with a convenient excuse for killing him. It would be better not to struggle. He spread his hands, showing that he was unarmed.

'Hepesh,' said the Doctor, 'there has been a terrible mistake. Let me explain!'

But Hepesh was not there to listen. As Grun deftly tied the Doctor's wrists with a silken cord, the High Priest stood closer, gloating before the Doctor's face.

'Alien!' spat the bearded priest. 'You have defiled the inner sanctum of the Temple of Aggedor. Your mind, your words, your being, all are evil!'

'You're being a fool, Hepesh,' snapped the Doctor. 'Let me speak to the king!'

'You go to him now,' replied the priest, 'It is his task to cast judgement upon you. But for what you have done, there is no defence, and only one punishment: your destruction! Grun, take him away!'

.        .        .        .        .

Ssorg had found no sign of Aggedor and had returned to Izlyr with only Jo's cloak in his great hands. It had been torn to shreds as though by a wild animal.

Without further discussion, Jo had been taken back to the Martian quarters for interrogation. Strangely enough, she felt less afraid than angry. To her, it was obvious that Izlyr already thought her guilty of some terrible crime.

'I tell you I saw the monster—he was there,' she insisted. 'You heard him, too, and you can see what he did to my cloak!'

'Ssorg, what else did you find?' demanded the warlord.

'Nothing, Lord Izlyr.'

'I'm not making it up,' cried Jo. 'Those cries—my cloak —why won't you believe the evidence?'

'True, we heard sounds,' admitted Izlyr with chilling preciseness, 'and we discovered your torn cloak. But only you have seen this monster—not us. It could be a clever trick!'

'It isn't!' exclaimed Jo furiously. 'I'm telling you the truth!'

'Yet you also entered our room, secretly. It was you that Ssorg found holding the servo-unit belonging to Arcturus. And you did not wait to be questioned as an innocent person would. You escaped!' accused Izlyr.

'I found Arcturus' thingumajig—in your room! It was you that must've taken it! And I escaped so that I could tell the Doctor and King Peladon!'

Izlyr didn't answer immediately. He studied Jo's face and paced before her, thinking. Eventually, he spoke.

'So, you believe that we tried to kill Arcturus.'

'If not, what was that servo-unit doing locked away in your room?' retorted Jo.

'Placed there by you, Princess, to cause trouble,' hissed the Martian.

'That's just not true!' cried Jo. 'We discovered Arcturus, nearly dead!'

There was a pause. Jo waited for Izlyr to rage with anger but instead he gave a dry staccato cough, a sound that she later came to understand as the Martian equivalent of a laugh.

'You are mistaken,' continued the warlord. 'Nobody tried to kill Arcturus.'

Jo blinked. 'What?'

'To kill a creature like Arcturus, the helium regenerator must be de-activated,' hissed the Martian. 'This was not attempted.'

'But . . .' Jo groped for the question, her mind racing, '—the missing unit . . .'

'Merely sensor equipment,' said Izlyr. 'Disconnection only produces a metabolic coma.'

75

'You mean . . . it couldn't be fatal?'

'Only uncomfortable,' whispered Izlyr.

For a moment, Jo was speechless. When at last she spoke, it was with a genuine note of apology in her voice.

'I'm sorry,' she said, 'it looks as if we've misjudged you, Izlyr. But the Doctor only knows your planet as bearing a race of warriors.'

'That was so—once,' conceded the Martian warlord. 'But we have learned to reject violence, except in self-defence.'

Jo pointed at Ssorg's arm, and the strange weapon there. 'What about Ssorg's gun? This is supposed to be a peaceful mission, isn't it?'

'Unfortunately, in order to spread peace, it is necessary to survive.'

Jo nodded. She could see the point. But she was still puzzled. 'If it wasn't you, who was it? Who could possibly benefit from all this troublemaking?'

Izlyr had no chance to offer any theories. With a flurry of tentacles, Alpha Centauri entered the room, and squeaked in panic: 'Izlyr—Ssorg—Princess—come quickly! The Doctor has been taken prisoner! He is in the throne room. We must go to him. He is on trial for his life!'

. . . . .

Peladon prepared to speak. He had heard Hepesh out and the essential fact of the Doctor's presence in the sacred temple could not be denied. The time had come, therefore, for judgement to be cast.

'Doctor, Federation delegates,' Peladon said, his face clearly showing his unhappiness at the situation, 'the charge is extreme sacrilege. You are accused—by Hepesh the High Priest and his witness Grun, the King's Champion—of desecrating our holy of holies, the Inner Sanctum of the Temple of Aggedor. Even as supreme ruler, I have no alternative. To this charge, the laws of Peladon allow of no defence, and of one punishment alone—death!'

Jo, watching the Doctor face the court with a quiet

76

dignity, bit back a cry at Peladon's doom-laden words. It had been explained to her that any interference, verbal or otherwise, would only make matters worse. Hepesh had ensured that none of the delegates had been given the chance to discuss the case with the Doctor. But now, at last, came his chance to speak.

'Your Majesty,' declared the Doctor with complete sincerity, 'there was no sacrilege intended. I assure you of that!'

'Only the death of the intruder can purify the sacred temple of Aggedor!' cried the High Priest.

The Doctor was prepared to explain—if he got the chance. 'You see, I had no idea that the tunnel would lead there.'

Peladon threw a sharp glance at his High Priest, and leaned forward. 'I know of no tunnels, Hepesh.'

'Both Hepesh and Grun know that below this citadel there exists a whole network of secret passages,' insisted the Doctor. 'But I doubt if he'll admit the fact.'

'Why should I admit to what doesn't exist?' sneered Hepesh. 'The alien is lying. There are no tunnels!'

The Doctor turned to the young king. 'King Peladon, I swear to you that I'm telling the truth. I'm innocent!'

'He was there,' growled Hepesh. 'Not only did he gaze upon the holy image, but he laid his foul alien hands upon him! Is this innocence? No! There is but one consequence, Majesty. Name it!'

Jo could keep silent no longer. 'He *is* innocent! You must believe him!'

Izlyr stood forward proudly. Jo held her breath. What would he say? With one word, he could eliminate the Doctor as an enemy of his race, and yet remain outside the event as a guiltless bystander. But his words surprised her.

'Peladon, this Earthling is a stranger to your planet. His ignorance of the law deserves consideration.'

'The crime is too great!' snapped Hepesh quickly.

'Then a royal pardon would count all the more highly with the Federation,' whispered Izlyr.

Hepesh was quick to interject again, his tongue as sharp

as his wits. 'The Federation cannot over-ride our holy laws!' he declared boldly. 'Such action is forbidden by its Charter of Freedoms!'

Arcturus, silent until now, glided forward slightly.

'That is correct,' the metallic voice confirmed. 'The Galactic Articles of Peace, paragraph 59, subsection 2 . . .'

'The law is against us,' wailed Alpha Centauri. 'We are powerless to interfere!'

'The law isn't always right,' cried Jo. 'You can't just let an innocent man be executed!'

'No one can prevent it, Earthling,' murmured Hepesh smugly, then turned to his king. 'Let it be done.'

But Jo was not yet beaten. Pushing her way past Hepesh, she threw herself at the foot of the throne, her desperate face uptilted to the young king sitting there. Their eyes met, as Jo put all her pleading into words.

'A king can do anything,' she said firmly, then dropped her voice so that her plea was directed to Peladon as a person, not as a royal judge. 'You asked me once if I believed in you. I want to. Well, if you honestly believe in peace, if you really despise violence and cruelty, this is your chance to prove it. Izlyr gave you the opportunity just now to offer a royal pardon. Think what an effect that would have on the Galactic Commission! But more than that—*I'm* asking you . . . as a friend, a person.' She paused, slightly breathless. She was sure there was a new kindness in his eyes; she was certain he would respond. 'You want to show yourself a civilised king,' she said, 'then do it . . .'

The brief strand of friendship and warmth was severed by the sharp tones of Hepesh's grim voice. 'The king can do nothing,' he insisted. 'He is bound by ancient law.'

The face of the young king saddened perceptibly. He knew that by rejecting Jo's plea he would lose all claim to her friendship. But he was helpless.

'Hepesh is right,' he said flatly. 'I am powerless. The laws of my people must stand.'

Hepesh moved forward to pull Jo back from the throne, but still she begged Peladon to act with mercy.

'Peladon . . . please!' she cried, 'there has to be some other way!'

Looking down at Jo's sweet face, so near to tears and yet so brave, a blinding memory bright as a revelation burst upon the young king's mind. It wasn't Jo's features that he saw before him, but those of his mother, Ellua. It was her voice, not Jo's, that spoke to him. And yet the words were the same. 'There has to be another way . . .' It had been a trivial incident, a moment's misuse of power by a boy not yet able to understand that his words held life and death for his people. A word of command and the servant would have been slain; but at his mother's quick intercession, he had held his hand, and decreed a far lesser punishment. Years later, that same servant had died, valiantly defending his royal master against a ravening wolf; a life given up willingly to a purpose—not wasted by a moment's thoughtless anger. The memory came and went in an instant—but it left the knowledge of the one harsh remedy that lay in the young king's power.

'There is an alternative,' declared the king, standing and facing the Doctor. 'Trial by combat.'

To the Doctor, the alternative that Peladon now offered was virtually a reprieve; at least, it meant that he had a fighting chance. To Jo, it seemed to offer the difference between the hangman's rope and the executioner's axe. Hepesh, on the other hand, saw Peladon's decree as a weakening of the throne's authority and yet another concession to the aliens.

'The alternative cannot stand!' he exclaimed. 'This alien is not of noble blood!'

'It's barbaric . . . !' Jo protested angrily. She had expected a royal pardon.

'It is all I can offer,' said the young king. Couldn't Jo see that he done as much as he dared?

Hepesh had not been answered. His objection still stood, and he reaserted it. 'The Earth delegate cannot be allowed an honourable alternative!'

Peladon was becoming irritated by Hepesh's constant and petty objections. He snapped back icily.

'You forget, Hepesh, that the Chairman Delegate is a man of rank and, as such, an honorary nobleman of the Citadel!' He turned to the Doctor. 'What do you say, Doctor?'

The Doctor met the young king's gaze proudly, and lifting his head, smiled. 'I accept the challenge, your majesty. Who do I fight?'

The king's next words tightened the band of fear around Jo's heart, and wiped the smile from the Doctor's face.

'You will be held captive in your room until dawn. Then you will enter the Pit of Combat and engage in a fight to the death—with Grun, the King's Champion!'

## 7

## Escape into Danger

The reassuring look from the Doctor as he was marched away had given Jo no comfort. Now the alien delegates had withdrawn to confer amongst themselves, and Jo had been shown to a room cut off from that in which the Doctor was being held. It was while she was sitting there, thinking desperately of ways to effect the Doctor's escape, that Grun knocked at her door and entered at her command. Seeing him there, Jo felt a moment of hope—he could only have been sent by the king. Had Peladon changed his mind? At Grun's mimed gesture that she should follow him, she smiled and did so, without any argument. She had to run to keep up with Grun's vast strides, and it was only a short time later that she once more stood before Peladon.

Her heart sank at Peladon's next command.

'Go, Grun,' he ordered. 'Prepare for the combat in honour of the Royal Beast.'

Grun saluted, bowed, and left. When the throne room

doors closed after him, Jo and Peladon were left alone together. Jo could hide her anger no longer. 'Why have you had me brought here?' she asked. 'To show me how clever you are at giving stupid orders?'

'I had to talk to you—' pleaded Peladon.

Jo wasn't impressed. 'Don't expect me to believe you, your . . . majesty,' she replied sarcastically, shaking her head in a firm negative when the young king indicated that she should be seated beside the throne.

'I'm sorry . . .' murmured Peladon, 'but there are some things I cannot change . . . even for you.'

'Did you ever want to? What do mercy and compassion mean to you? You need someone to die to justify your stupid superstition!'

Peladon stiffened. No one normally offered a rebuke like this to the throne and remained free. Were Hepesh here now, he would be quick to act on the old harsh laws. Jo did not know that by allowing her to spill her understandable anger against the king without witness, he was protecting her life.

'I want no one to die,' he said. 'I've done all I can. I've given the Doctor the only chance that lay in my power.'

Jo turned away, too moved even to sneer. Peladon saw this, and waited—but made no move to comfort her. She was so like Ellua, he thought. Grief brought out the warrior in her soul and she would defend the Doctor to the end.

'He means a great deal to you, this Doctor,' the king observed.

She nodded. 'Yes . . . he does.'

'I respect him as a man,' admitted the king. 'And I have no reason to call him my enemy.' At this, Jo turned, her face ever hopeful; but Peladon raised his hand to check what he knew she would say. 'But please—do not hate me for being forced to do my duty as a king.'

'But I don't hate you,' said Jo, irritated. 'Why can't you see?'

'Let me explain,' interrupted the royal youth. 'Both Torbis and my father died before they could break the centuries of tradition that bind us. But my mother taught me all she could of those qualities she brought from her own planet, Earth: justice, compassion—and love. She knew the time would come—'

'Then make it now!' exclaimed Jo. 'Be the king she wanted you to be!' She paused. 'The king *I* want you to be ...'

'I cannot achieve that alone,' the king said, frankly.

'But that's what the Federation's for—they will help you!' cried Jo excitedly, not yet realising the line of Peladon's thought.

'They are outsiders—politicians,' he insisted. 'I need someone at my side with those same qualities that *she* had ...'

Suddenly, as the young king took her hand, Jo knew what he was getting at—and gaped, almost comically, in amazement. The question, when it came, was polite and formal.

'Princess ...' said Peladon gently, 'will you give your agreement to an interplanetry alliance—by marriage—to me?'

※          ·          ·          ·          ·

The Doctor was surprised. No sooner had he arrived in his room, than Hepesh had dismissed the armed escort. But listening to their feet march away into the distance, the Doctor suddenly understood what Hepesh was up to.

'Yes,' he mused aloud, 'you're a wily old bird, aren't you, Hepesh? The door will be left conveniently open—and I'll be killed while trying to escape. Is that it?'

'No one will stand in your way,' replied the High Priest.

'Which probably means an arrow in the back,' observed the Doctor drily. 'You do realise, don't you, that my death will certainly create an interplanetary scandal?'

'I know the consequences, alien,' answered Hepesh. 'And I do not want your death.' The Doctor frowned as Hepesh pointed to the open door. 'That is your route to freedom. Trust me, and take it. Leave this planet, and live!'

The offer was tempting, but the Doctor wasn't satisfied with the High Priest's apparent honesty. He decided to test just how far Hepesh was prepared to go in order to get rid of an unwanted guest, without violence.

'I'm afraid I can't, old chap,' apologised the Doctor. 'You see, I still haven't got my space shuttle back.'

'A blue box was found on the lower slopes of this mountain,' replied the High Priest. 'It is being brought to the Citadel now.'

'And what about the Princess Jo?' queried the Doctor, warily. Hepesh paused before answering.

'She will be allowed to leave with you, of course.'

Such a glib reply bothered the Doctor. Promises were easy if you didn't intend keeping them. Hepesh was almost too eager.

'But why go to all this trouble, old chap?' demanded the Doctor, shrewdly. 'You could simply have me killed . . .'

Hepesh faced him proudly. 'I don't want this planet destroyed in retaliation, by Federation warships. I seek only an honourable peace.'

'Yet you slap the Federation in the face,' said the Doctor, 'by sabotaging the Commission. Why?'

'Because I am afraid,' confessed the High Priest, not flinching from his opponent's stare, 'as you would be . . .'

Was he sincere, wondered the Doctor? Patriotism was often a genuine motive in driving men to commit the most violent acts to preserve their nation's freedom. If this was the case with Hepesh, he might have a point—though it still didn't make his methods anything but wrong.

'Afraid of what? Joining the Federation is a safeguard —a protection needed by a developing planet like yours.'

'That is not true!' retorted Hepesh sharply. 'I know the Federation's true intent!'

'Its only purpose is to help you,' insisted the Doctor.

'No!' cried the priest. 'If you think that, you are blind! They will exploit us for our minerals, enslave us with their machines, corrupt us with their glittering technology! The face of this planet will be changed. The past will be swept away!' He paused, his face tragic. 'Nothing that I know, or value, will remain . . .'

Yes, thought the Doctor, Hepesh is sincere all right. He's also highly dangerous. A fanatic set against progress. Obsessed with the traditions of the past, to the point where individual deaths are simply stepping stones to success. But was Hepesh alone in his campaign against the Federation? Somehow, the Doctor had to find out.

'My dear Hepesh,' remarked the Doctor condescendingly, 'the progress offered by the Federation isn't like that at all. And hiding behind the traditions of the past won't solve anything.'

'Our roots are in the past,' growled Hepesh. 'I would rather be a cave dweller, and free, than a city slave, civilised to the point of mindlessness!'

'Do you call holding your people prisoner by ritual and superstition, freedom?'

'The people need Aggedor. He is our protector!'

The Doctor smiled, tauntingly. He had to provoke the High Priest into admitting the truth. 'And do you seriously expect your pet ghost to take on the whole Federation single-handed? My dear chap, you haven't a hope!' The trick worked. Hepesh's eyes flared with anger.

'You are a fool, alien!' he snarled fiercely. 'We do not stand alone!'

'Oh . . . ?' queried the Doctor. 'And who exactly is standing with you?'

Hepesh did not answer. His eyes narrowed and his face grew bitter at finding himself caught out by the Doctor. When at last he spoke, he chose to ignore the Doctor's last question, as he moved to the doorway.

'Take your chance while you can, alien,' the High Priest snarled. 'It isn't long till dawn!'

.        .        .        .        .

Jo had left the throne room in something of a daze. She had not given Peladon an answer to his formal proposal of marriage. Despite his obvious sincerity, she couldn't be sure that his real purpose wasn't mainly political—and that was no basis for a wedding, in Jo's book! Walking back to the delegates' conference room, Jo reflected on Peladon's personality. She found him almost impossible to understand. One moment he was condemning the Doctor to certain death; the next he was proposing not just a marriage, but an interplanetry blood alliance!' To Jo, the events just couldn't be separated, but Peladon had insisted they had no connection. His judgement of the case against the Doctor fell under his duty as a king; his offer of marriage to Jo sprang from his feelings as a man. In spite of this, Jo couldn't help wondering what he would say if he ever discovered she wasn't of royal blood at all!

In her absence, the delegates were speculating about Jo's all too obvious attraction for Peladon. Although they didn't yet know of the proposal, they suspected that it was almost bound to happen, sooner or later. Arcturus, in particular was bitterly concerned that their mission was being so deliberately misused. 'The facts point to only one conclusion,' grated his mechanical voice. 'An attempt is being made to establish a unilateral blood alliance between the planets Peladon and Earth!'

Although sentimentally attracted to the idea, Alpha Centauri was confused by the related events. 'But if a marriage is to occur,' shrilled the over-excited hexapod, 'why is the Doctor to be executed?'

'It is unusual,' hissed Izlyr, 'to celebrate such an event with the execution of a planetary ambassador.'

Arcturus was not to be deflected from his theory.

'That is obviously designed to confuse us,' he said coldly. 'There is a conspiracy!'

'A conspiracy!' repeated Alpha Centauri, waving dark blue tentacles in panic. 'Izlyr—Arcturus—tell me what is happening. I do not understand!'

It was at this point in the discussion that Jo entered, and heard Arcturus' next ominous words.

'It is a plot to destroy Federation unity. If we remain, we shall be the next victims. We must withdraw from Peladon immediately!'

'No,' shouted Jo as she entered the room and heard

85

Arcturus's remark, 'you can't do that! What about the Doctor?'

Alpha Centauri was sympathetic—but cowardly. 'But Princess, we must leave—if only to avoid further violence. We cannot interfere in local politics. What would the Galactic Council say?'

'Probably that you've got no power to cancel the mission,' said Jo firmly, 'have you?'

Izlyr spoke thoughtfully. 'The Princess is correct. Federation authority is required. We cannot act alone.'

'We have full powers in an emergency,' rapped Arcturus. 'If we stay, we risk being taken as hostages, or worse. Such a situation calls for emergency procedures!'

'It's true,' wailed Alpha Centauri. 'We're in terrible danger! We must leave while we have the chance!'

'And leave the Doctor behind—to die?' stormed Jo. 'What sort of politicians *are* you? Cowards, the lot of you!'

'This is a very delicate political situation,' grated Arcturus. 'Your immature emotional response does not help.'

'Well, let me tell you,' retorted Jo, 'it'll be worse than delicate if the Doctor is killed! What will the Galactic Council say to *that*?'

It was Izlyr that gave the only possible answer to Jo's angry question. 'It would amount to a declaration of war. The Federation would be compelled to retaliate. The planet of Peladon would probably be destroyed.'

'Any action on our part could precipitate a worse conflict,' stated Arcturus. 'Therefore, we must do nothing to interfere!'

Jo could hardly believe her ears. Even when the so-called leader of the group was in deadly danger, they wouldn't raise a finger or a tentacle to save him! 'That's marvellous!' exclaimed Jo, scathingly. 'Your recipe for peace—do nothing, and let the other clods die! Well—thanks for nothing!'

And with that, she rushed blindly from the room.

The door to the Doctor's room was still open; but he remained inside. The guard captain that Hepesh had planted to observe the Doctor still waited, patiently lurking in the shadows. The moment the Doctor left his chamber and took advantage of Hepesh's offer of freedom, the captain was to report it immediately to the High Priest. He was beginning to wonder whether the alien intended to take his chance with Grun instead.

In fact, the Doctor was rather busy. As his deft fingers constructed the small but intricate device he needed for his journey, he studied the map that Hepesh had so thoughtfully left him. It showed a short, direct route to the entrance of the secret tunnel used by the Doctor previously. The route to the temple was indicated, but marked boldly with an 'X'. The Doctor smiled wryly: he wasn't likely to chance trespassing *there* again! The route shown on the map lead to an area marked 'BLUE BOX'. This, then, was where the TARDIS would be waiting—or would it? The Doctor had his own ideas about that. For now, it was enough to concentrate on reaching the secret passage. He stood, and considered the spinning, glittering construction he had just made. Yes, it should do the trick nicely. He stilled its movement, and slipped it into a convenient pocket. Then, without any attempt at concealment, he walked outside. A faint flicker of movement in the shadows brought a grim smile to his lean face. Hepesh didn't believe in leaving anything to chance, obviously. The hidden watcher would now report to the High Priest that the bait had been taken—and then what would Hepesh do, the Doctor wondered. Perhaps he wouldn't have to do anything. Perhaps what lay in store for the Doctor was already there in the tunnels, waiting. If it was, the Doctor thought, he was ready for it; and if he came through that meeting alive, he suspected he would know enough to make Peladon reject Hepesh, and see reason. *If*, he reminded himself, he came out of it alive . . .

The knock on Jo's door seemed to herald even more trouble. In fact, it was Izlyr and Ssorg who stood outside, and they didn't look any more threatening than usual. 'What do you want?' demanded Jo, irritably.

'I wish to talk with you,' whispered Izlyr. 'May we enter?'

'Be my guest,' said Jo acidly, and moved into the room. Izlyr and Ssorg entered and closed the door, then stood, slightly uneasily, Jo thought. 'Well?' she demanded.

'You left the meeting in anger,' observed the warlord.

'There wasn't much else I could do, once you lot had ganged up on the Doctor!' retorted Jo.

'Your assumption is incorrect, Princess. We have not, as you call it, ganged up. Each delegate has his own position to justify. A free discussion is inevitable.'

'I know, I was there,' observed Jo caustically. 'It was a matter of who was going to run away first, wasn't it?'

'Arcturus is a coward by logic,' explained the Martian, 'and Alpha Centauri is a coward by instinct. Nevertheless, they will not leave the Doctor stranded.'

Jo looked at the proud Martian with surprise, and a small spark of hope brightened her face. 'Why the sudden change of heart?' she asked.

Izlyr turned his mask-like face to her. It betrayed no emotion, but for some reason Jo felt that the Ice Warrior was undeniably pleased with himself.

'The emergency law that Arcturus was so quick to quote can only operate under unanimous decision. I voted to stay.'

Jo couldn't hide her amazement. 'What!' Her mind raced. Was one of the Doctor's most feared enemies going to defend him?

'When the statue of the Royal Beast was made to fall,' explained Izlyr, 'the Doctor saved my life. Now, I intend to save his.'

'Izlyr—that's wonderful!' shouted Jo, then stopped, frowning. 'But . . . how?'

The conversation that followed would not normally be heard, outside a room such as Jo's. Thick-walled, and with a massive wooden door, the room's acoustics would not carry Jo's light voice and Izlyr's hoarse whisper to the casual eavesdropper. But where the human ear is a fallible instrument, the highly refined aural sensors that had been developed on Arcturus for its delegate's information processes, were infinitely more effective. The monitoring input mike that Arcturus had placed against the outside of Jo's door picked up and relayed every movement, every breath, every word that was spoken within. The information so obtained, fed into the micro-computerised decision-making centre of the neuroplasm, was processed instantaneously and a plan formed . . .

'We have already been to the Doctor's room to acquaint him with our decision,' hissed the Martian warlord; 'but when we arrived, his door was open and he was not there.'

'The Doctor's escaped !' cried Jo.

'It would seem to be so,' whispered Izlyr. 'The map he left behind indicates that he has gone to ground in the secret tunnels beneath the citadel.'

'Of course !' exclaimed Jo, 'and I bet I know just where, too !'

'That is what I hoped. You must go to him, and bring him to the throne room to face the king. Peladon must be made to understand the truth !'

Jo wasn't so sure. 'But why not let him escape ?'

'By escaping, he will appear to be a common criminal,' hissed Izlyr. 'By throwing himself on the king's mercy—plus the case that I will put forward for the Federation—the king will act accordingly.'

'To tell the truth,' wondered Jo, 'I wouldn't have been surprised if that's what's in his mind, too . . .'

'Then go to him, Princess,' insisted Izlyr. 'He will listen to you.' As Jo nodded, he gestured to Ssorg, who stepped forward and presented her with the map. 'Here is the map that will lead you to him. We will meet you in the throne room. But do not delay . . .'

By the time they left Jo's room, Arcturus was nowhere to be seen.

The secret door leading to the castle corridor closed behind him, and the Doctor found himself once more beneath the castle stones. He smiled : the place was becoming quite familiar! He quickly followed the line of wall torches to the limit of their run, then paused. By a simple trick of concentration, he visualised the map in minute detail. Yes, it was the next turning on the left. He moved on, confidently picking up the dim glow of the phosphor streak, and soon his eyes became accustomed to the dim but constant light. Before long, he had come to the point where, according to Hepesh's map, the TARDIS should be. It wasn't there. The Doctor smiled to himself, grimly. He'd thought as much. Hepesh really was a tricky customer—but things weren't so bad if you were prepared. The Doctor took out the gleaming device that he had made. It'd be just as well to have it ready to hand. He was pleased to find that it not only picked up the phosphor glow, but magnified it to an unusual intensity. Then, tightening his grip upon it for reassurance, he strode on.

The message had reached Hepesh in the temple, and he frowned. A change of plan at this late stage was dangerous—the trap the Doctor had entered so willingly was deadly enough. And even if he had the luck to return alive, who would believe him? But the message was clear : the Doctor was to be hunted, his escape officially made known and, when he was discovered, it would be as Torbis had been found : dead. Hepesh called the guard captain to him, and gave the necessary commands. 'Take your men and search all the known tunnels and catacombs beneath the citadel. The alien is armed and dangerous, and will neither expect nor grant mercy. You will bring back his corpse as proof.'

The captain nodded and knelt for blessing beneath Hepesh's ringed hand.

'Aggedor go with you,' said Hepesh. The hunt was on.

The ringing howl that came from the shadows ahead made the Doctor pause in his stride—but it confirmed his theory about Hepesh. It wasn't the TARDIS that was to be his meeting place with Jo. It had been an obvious and simple trap. The map had been deliberately drawn to lead him straight to Aggedor, the Royal Beast. That dreadful cry roared forth again, terrifying in its resonance through the confines of the gloomy tunnel. Yes, thought the Doctor, this was to be the moment of truth. Well, so be it. Then, as the great shaggy bulk of the Royal Beast moved forward out of the shadows that had kept its full horror from the Doctor's sight, it roared again. Raising the spinning mirror of the device that was his only defence, the Doctor spoke with quiet intensity.

'So there you are, old chap. I rather thought I'd be meeting up with you . . .'

# 8

# Trial by Combat

'Lord Izlyr,' whispered the great warrior Ssorg to his master, 'there is something unusual about the Doctor's escape.'

'For an Earthling,' hissed Izlyr, 'the Doctor has a brain of considerable quality.' He stopped in his stride, and Ssorg halted also. 'Why do you say unusual, Ssorg?'

'To escape alone is ingenious, but when we found him, there were no guards.'

Izlyr considered this: Ssorg was right. In their haste to explain the situation to the Earth Princess, the point had escaped his attention. What was the explanation?

'Perhaps the guard left his post to follow the Doctor,' suggested Izlyr. 'It would be his duty to recapture the prisoner.'

'But no alarm has been raised, Lord Izlyr,' discreetly pointed out Ssorg. 'Why should that be?'

'He has been allowed to escape! There can only be one purpose in such a plan.'

'To kill him,' agreed Ssorg, dispassionately. 'But what

*The spinning mirror flashed its pattern of reflected light
into the creature's eyes.*

about the princess? She has gone to find him in the palace catacombs. She, too, will be in danger.'

'But she has the only map!' said Izlyr. 'We cannot hope to find her without help.' He made his decision in an instant. 'We will demand help from Peladon and Hepesh. If they refuse, they will have much to answer for!'

.     .     .     .     .

Aggedor was still. The eyes that had glared so murderously at the Doctor were glued to the mirror of the Doctor's device which was spinning a rhythmic pattern of reflected light across the monster's tusked face. The Doctor's droning voice added to the hypnotic effect of the whirling disc, as it murmured strange, simple words to an irresistible tune ... The Doctor stopped chanting, but let the spinning mirror continue to flash its pattern of reflected phosphor light into the creature's eyes, now languid in relaxation. 'Well, Aggedor old chap,' chuckled the Doctor, 'You seem to be very partial to Venusian lullabies, don't you ...'

As though in reply, the normally fearsome monster growled, but with pleasure, like a contented cat. It was crouched on all fours, its great, powerful bulk completely relaxed. The mirror disc still holding its attention, the Doctor moved gently closer. His movements were almost imperceptible, but at last he was close enough to fondle the ears and forehead of the mighty beast. The light, though dim, was bright enough for the Doctor to see the details of the terrifying head : the matted hair, the nose tusk, white and gleaming, and the glistening fangs set into the huge, cruel jaws. The great beast, delighting in the light and the soothing fingers scratching its head, stretched slowly; and from the corner of his eye, the Doctor caught sight of the fearsome claws that had struck down the frail figure of Torbis. Distracted for a moment, he lowered the mirror—and immediately Aggedor roared with irritation. The Doctor hastily set the disc in speedier motion, letting the miniature strobe effect fall across the creature's eyeline; then sighed in relief as its anger subsided once again. He cleared his throat, nervously, and chuckled.

'I think we'd better have another chorus, don't you?' he murmured. 'Best not get too friendly, had I? Not until you're properly under, that is . . .' And he started his soothing chant once more.

.     .     .     .     .

The terrifying roar had made Jo freeze in her tracks. Aggedor! But if Aggedor was up ahead, thought Jo, so was the Doctor. And if he was in trouble, now was *not* the time to desert him. Gathering up all her courage, she ran forward into the half-darkness. Turning a bend in the tunnel, she stopped again, and barely stifled a scream : the Doctor seemed to be lying between Aggedor's outstretched paws! Whatever weapon it was that the Doctor was wielding, it looked so puny as to be useless for dealing with the animal which was slavering over him! Added to which, the Doctor was giving out a low and painful moaning sound, as though in agony from a terrible wound. Without a weapon of her own, there was little she could do—but at least she had the advantage of surprise. With a great, brave cry, she charged to the Doctor's rescue.

'It's alright, Doctor—I'm coming—I'll save you!'

'Jo! No! Keep back!' the Doctor shouted—but it was too late.

Aggedor, startled from his semi-daze by Jo's frightening shouts and screams, lumbered to his feet and lurched away into the darkness of the lower tunnels. Jo, uncomprehending, clutched the Doctor—and was rather put out when he pushed her irritably away.

'Jo, you idiot! Just when I'd started to get through to him!'

Jo stood gaping at the Doctor. What he'd just said didn't make sense. Perhaps he was in a bad state of shock.

'What? What are you talking about?'

The Doctor held up the mirror device and, with a flick of his fingers, set it spinning.

'I'm talking about Aggedor—and this,' he snapped. 'It's a form of technical hypnosis.'

'You don't mean . . . you were actually *talking* to it?'

'Not talking, Jo, but a form of communication, nevertheless: empathy.'

'Empathy,' Jo repeated, in a strangely dull voice.

'Yes, it's a variation on animal telepathy.' He stopped, and realised that Jo, too, had succumbed to the spell of the spinning disc. Her eyes were wide open, but she could obviously see nothing. Her mouth was fixed in a vaguely pleasurable smile. At the sharp click of the Doctor's fingers, and his word of command, she blinked back into a dazed consciousness.

'Jo? Jo! Oh, good grief, wake up!'

Jo looked up at the Doctor. She didn't understand. 'Doctor . . . what happened?'

'You've just ruined a very promising experiment,' he replied dryly, 'that's what happened!'

'I'm sorry,' said Jo angrily. 'I was only trying to help you! I thought you were going to be killed!

'And very brave you were too, Jo,' the Doctor replied with a smile. 'But my meeting with our friend Aggedor wasn't entirely wasted. Come on—let's go and find King Peladon. There are one or two things I think he ought to know . . .'

⁂    •    •    •    •

Izlyr, backed by Ssorg, was being unusually abrupt with the king. Peladon seemed confused by the events that Izlyr described. Hepesh remained cool and said little. The warlord sensed a hint of desperation in the king's voice.

'But if the Doctor isn't in his room,' queried Peladon, 'where is he?'

'In the tunnels beneath the citadel,' insisted the Martian. 'But I believe his journey was a trap!'

'Tunnels?' remarked Hepesh in disbelief. 'There are no tunnels.

'We found a map,' hissed the warlord, 'with secret

routes marked to the temple. This will prove the Doctor's story.'

'If such a map exists,' remarked the High Priest, 'it will prove that he is a spy. *I* know of no tunnel—but if he had a map his plea of innocence must be false!'

'Delegate Izlyr,' requested the king, 'where is this map? Show me.'

'It is in the hands of the Earth Princess,' declared the Martian. 'She is using it to find the Doctor.'

'They run away like common criminals!' cried Hepesh. 'Let both their lives be forfeit. Let them be hunted and destroyed! They do not deserve an honourable death.'

Suddenly a familiar voice rang out.

'Sorry to disappoint you, Hepesh, but I'm requesting a personal audience with the king.'

'Guards!' shouted the High Priest, with an imperious gesture. 'Kill them!'

Before the guards could raise their swords against Jo or the Doctor, the king spoke out.

'Wait!' he ordered. 'The king commands you to wait!'

The guards fell back. Peladon turned his troubled face towards the Doctor.

'Your majesty,' said the Doctor pleasantly, 'I bring you a message ... from Aggedor, the Royal Beast.'

Hepesh whirled to confront the king. He pointed a condemning finger at the Doctor. 'The alien commits ever greater sacrilege! No one sees Aggedor and lives!'

'Well, I did,' commented the Doctor. 'And I must say, I found him very pleasant company—for an animal.' He looked about him shrewdly at the consternation caused by this remark, then added. 'He didn't even seem to mind when I scratched him behind the ears ...'

Hepesh was almost beside himself with fury. 'The Earthling defiles all that is sacred to us! He must be silenced!'

'Yes, old chap,' remarked the Doctor, 'that'd suit you very well, wouldn't it?'

Izlyr spoke up. 'Let us hear what the Doctor has to say, your majesty.'

96

'No!' cried Hepesh.

All eyes turned to the throne. 'We will hear him, Hepesh.'

The Doctor smiled gratefully, and approached the throne.

'Thank you, your majesty,' he said. 'I have seen for myself that Aggedor is no ghost or spirit—but a truly magnificent beast, fit to be called royal. I also know that his power is being used falsely : to destroy any future you may have as a member of the Galactic Federation!'

'You lie!' exclaimed Hepesh. 'His manifestation is holy, and he will take a terrible revenge!'

'Rubbish,' clipped the Doctor. 'That manifestation, as you call it, is solid, hairy fact!'

'It's true!' protested Jo. 'It isn't a ghost—I've seen it, too.'

'Then produce this creature!' sneered the High Priest.

'We can, if his majesty will permit it,' said the Doctor confidently. 'Aggedor lives in the tunnels beneath this palace...'

The king looked doubtful. 'You spoke of tunnels before, Doctor. They are a mystery to me ... and to Hepesh.'

'That's what *he* says,' commented Jo.

'Hepesh gave me a map, your majesty,' the Doctor said, 'showing not only the secret entrance to the catacombs, but the route which I took by accident to the temple.'

'I gave this alien no map,' denied the High Priest vehemently. But his eyes were afraid.

The Doctor turned to Jo, and held out his hand. 'Where is it, Jo? Let's show his majesty the directions for my escape—in Hepesh's own handwriting.'

Jo looked at him in dismay. Her empty hands showed that she no longer had the precious map.

'Doctor ... I'm sorry ...' she said. 'I must've dropped it when I had a go at Aggedor.'

'A search must be organised!' hissed Izlyr.

'They have nothing!' cried Hepesh. 'No proof to substantiate their foul lies! And now they demand time—for what? To postpone the trial by combat! It is another alien trick ! Do not listen to them, majesty.'

'Once I've proved that Aggedor is alive, the trial by combat won't be necessary,' retorted the Doctor.

'Indeed,' sneered the jubilant High Priest. 'And you will spend a lifetime looking for these mythical tunnels ! No—it is a coward's excuse ! Let him be taken to the Pit !'

'No !' cried Jo, appealing to Peladon, whose face was clouded by a deep sadness.

'Let him face his challenger !' declared Hepesh fiercely.

Jo could only beg with her eyes. The king gave her no reason for hope.

'I am sorry, Doctor,' the young king said despondently, 'you offer me not proof, but mere words. The combat must go on. Take him away.'

. . . . .

At Izlyr's request, Peladon had allowed Ssorg to accompany the Doctor to the armoury and guardroom to be kitted out for combat. It had seemed a puzzling, even innocent, favour, but Jo was grateful to the Martian for suggesting it. At least it protected the Doctor from any more of the High Priest's deadly tricks. Izlyr had stalked back to the delegates' room, not trying to conceal his cold anger. He had managed to prevent Arcturus and Alpha Centauri from pulling out of the Federation mission, but there was little else he could do by himself. Could he persuade the other two delegates to present Peladon with a firm ultimatum? It seemed most unlikely. Jo, too, had risky plans of her own : she had decided to tackle Grun, the King's Champion, face to face. When she got to his official quarters, she found the room empty and the door unlocked. She was about to turn away when her eye caught the gleam of brightly polished armour, and she looked more closely. There, on a ceremonial stand, was a complete set of superbly worked bronze accoutrements —so magnificent, they had to be the trappings that Grun would be wearing in the coming combat. Set on its stand, the armour matched Grun's size more or less exactly. Jo stood in awe before the empty shell that Grun would soon inhabit. The mask of Aggedor had been moulded in high relief on the great breastplate. It was terrible to behold. Each plate on the loose skirt which girdled the hips bore its own cruel design, as did the shin guards and gauntlets. Towering above the whole was the helmet. Its peaked brow, low over the wearer's eyes and linked with the heavy nose guard and cheek straps, formed a mask more terrifying than that of Aggedor himself. The blood-red crest of horse hair that topped the helmet would make Grun seem even more huge than he was already. Jo gulped as she thought of the Doctor confronted by this armoured tank of a man—David and Goliath, and no mistake! A sudden, wordless grunt of anger made her turn. There, standing in the doorway, was Grun.

Jo took a deep breath, and didn't flinch. She hadn't come to play the coward. That'd be too easy. Grun, even without his armour, and dressed only in the knee-length tunic that went beneath it, looked every inch the warrior. He pointed first at Jo then the doorway. The message was clear—she must go! But Jo made no attempt to leave. She not only stood her ground but pointed to the carpet before her, and commanded Grun to kneel. Her face took on a regal bearing and her gestures were correspondingly decisive. Fortunately, Grun would never know that her knees were wobbling like jelly, and that if he had shouted at her, she would probably have run and hidden behind his suit of armour in the corner! He didn't shout, however. At the sharp tone of her voice, all the training of a soldier subservient to the royal line responded . . . and he knelt.

'Grun,' said Jo, gaining confidence at this admission of respect, 'you are a brave and honourable soldier—but you are being misled. Hepesh has tricked you with false words. I am here to tell you the truth. You will listen . . . and you may rise,' Jo added hastily.

Grun stood up, his mighty form rigidly at the attention. Jo tried to remember what the Brigadier, or Mike would say to a lower rank. 'At ease,' she said crisply, and Grun relaxed.

When Jo looked at him again, she almost burst out laughing. His face expressed wonderment that such a slip of a girl should have the stuff of generals in her. She decided not to overdo the sergeant-major bit : friendly persuasion was what she was here for, and she had to make it good.

'Grun,' she said. 'I am entrusting you with a secret that only I and your King Peladon share . . .' She paused, and tried to work out what she had to say next, without actually telling an out-and-out lie. 'Peladon has asked me to be his royal bride—' She was about to continue, but found that Grun was once more kneeling at her feet. When she looked into his face, it was full of genuine pleasure. He took her hand and placed it on his head, a sign that he would serve her as faithfully as his present master. Jo was slightly alarmed. She hadn't said 'yes' yet, but everybody seemed to take it for granted that she would! 'Such an alliance,' she said, 'would bring the planet of Peladon and the planet Earth very close . . .'

Grun looked, if anything, more pleased. But his face fell at Jo's next words.

'Unfortunately,' declared Jo, 'this union is doomed before it has begun. The man that you are to fight in mortal combat—the Doctor—,' Jo placed her hand behind her back and crossed her fingers to cancel out the bold untruth, 'is the only person of rank who can grant consent for it to happen! By killing him, you will destroy any chance of wedlock between me and your king. And I think you are aware that will make your royal lord . . . quite desperately unhappy.' Watch it, Jo, she thought to herself. You're beginning to sound as grand and toffee-nosed as Queen Elizabeth the First! In spite of that, it looked as if her words had struck home. Grun's face was genuinely sad, and the noise he made pathetic in its pleading. She followed the direction of his pointing hand, and knew the cause of his unhappiness. He was indicating the miniature shrine in one corner of his room. In that shrine was a statue—of Aggedor.

Jo took a deep breath—this was the real crunch.

'I know you are dedicated to Aggedor,' she said, 'and you have seen his face—and lived. But you do not know that both I and the Doctor have looked upon Aggedor as well.'

Grun looked at her with something approaching awe— and then she caught just a shade of suspicion at the back of his eyes. She'd have to be careful.

'He has not slain us, as you can see,' she said. 'But he is angry . . . and disturbed. His ways are being twisted by the very man who should be his greatest servant— Hepesh!'

At this, Grun gave a great, troubled sigh, and hid his face in his hands. As protector of the throne, his life had been uncomplicated—until the arrival of these aliens. Now, he was faced with a clash of loyalties : should he serve his king, with whom he knew Hepesh disagreed, or the High Priest and the voice of Aggedor? If, by executing the Doctor, he destroyed the marriage that the king desired, he would be like dust in Peladon's eyes. But if he broke his bond, and defied the command of Hepesh, the consequences would be terrible indeed. For Hepesh had the power to call down the very form of Aggedor and, in a moment, he, the King's Champion, would suffer the fate of Torbis. Queen or not, this Earthling princess had no power to prevent that. He looked into her eyes, and knew what he must do. But his decision was not to be made known. Hepesh was standing in the doorway, and his gaze was like fire.

'Princess,' the High Priest's voice cracked like a whip, 'I know your mind. You think that you can lure the King's Champion from the task that awaits him—but you are too late !' His command shifted to Grun, who stood alert and waiting. 'Make ready, Grun. The hour has come !'

　　　＊　　　　＊　　　　＊　　　　＊　　　　＊

Ssorg indicated the various pieces of armour hanging ready for use, and whispered urgently, 'Prepare yourself, Doctor. You will need this primitive protection.'

The Doctor glanced at the breast plates and leg guards,

and shook his head. They were heavy and well made—but little use against an axe or sword wielded by someone the size of Grun.

'They'll only slow me down, Ssorg,' he said firmly. 'What I need most is speed. Grun's a trained warrior, and pretty deadly, I don't doubt. I'm no match for him in a straight slogging match, so I'll have to play it my way . . .' He smiled at what must have been consternation in Ssorg's mind. 'I think I'll give him a few surprises. Don't worry . . .'

'But, this Grun . . .' hissed Ssorg, '*he* will have armour. How can you hope to harm him? My people have long known that great strength in defence, added to superior fire-power, is essential to victory in battle.'

'I knew your ancestors well, old chap,' murmured the Doctor drily. 'They were great warriors, bred for battle, and you're the culmination of their greatest qualities. That isn't so with me. I've come to discover that brute force isn't always the answer,' he smiled, 'and now's my chance to prove it!'

'You are brave,' hissed the puzzled Ice Warrior, 'but you are foolish. Perhaps you are skilled in the use of Pel weapons?' he added hopefully.

'I'll have no idea until I get to the Pit, old chap,' said the Doctor cheerfully, taking off his cloak and folding it neatly. Ssorg took it from him. He also slipped out of his elegant jacket, and handed it to Ssorg for safe-keeping. Still strikingly elegant in his ruffled shirt and dark trews, the Doctor now had a freedom of movement. But to a trained soldier like Ssorg, he looked ridiculously vulnerable, like an insect to be swept aside and crushed.

'At least take a suitable weapon of your own,' insisted the Martian. 'A laser pistol would destroy Grun and end the fight in seconds!'

'The combat has to be on their terms, I'm afraid,' pointed out the Doctor. 'The weapons to be used are waiting for us in the Pit, and I'll doubt if there'll be anything as sophisticated as that sonic gun of yours, Ssorg.' The Doctor indicated the small but deadly sonic impulse destructor that was an integral part of the Ice Warrior's forearm.

'Grun will kill you,' replied the Martian, fatefully.

'He's got to catch me, first,' retorted the Doctor. 'Float like the butterfly, sting like the bee,' he quoted, with a wry smile and his own variation of the Ali shuffle, 'so let's see what Grun will make of that!'

．　　　．　　　．　　　．　　　．

Alone in the temple, Peladon stood before the mighty image of the Royal Beast, its stern face seeming to shift and ripple in the drifting smoke of the incense burners. In the old days, the king would come here to pray, to seek guidance, or ask for reassurance for his own decisions. Now, Peladon had a dedication of a very different kind, and one for which, if Hepesh was right, the young king would be forever damned.

'Oh, Aggedor,' began Peladon, then stopped. Angrily, he realised he was confronting a being that, in all intelligence, he knew could not exist in any form other than an image. He was trying to communicate with a figment of Hepesh's warped mind! How can I ever hope to be a progressive ruler, he thought bitterly, if part of me is still bound up with the deepest superstitions of my backward people? Perhaps never, came his mind's reply. But he could at least take the first step and release himself from the bondage of irrational belief. Peladon raised his face to the stone image yet again, but there was no fear or weakness in his voice now. When he spoke, it was to an equal.

'Aggedor, you have cast this fear upon us, hear me, Peladon of Peladon, whom it is your duty to guide and protect. Your wisdom is that of the savage. Your retribution in my name is barbaric. Your title, once honoured, is now another name for Death. I say there shall be no more killing in your name. This dawn, an alien will fight for his life, challenged by your ancient law. If he dies, understand this: all images of Aggedor shall be cast down, and your shrines and temples walled up with the heaviest stones. All mention of your name shall be forbidden!'

Peladon paused. If he was to be struck down for sacrilege, now was the moment. Nothing happened. He took breath, and went on, 'But if the alien lives—even at the cost of my Champion's life—then shall the name of Aggedor be honoured and respected once more in the land of Peladon as a bringer of peace and good fortune.' The young king bowed and saluted in the traditional manner, then, straightening, ended his edict : 'So be it.' And as he spoke, he saw the figure of Hepesh step forward from the shadows into the torchlight. The old man's face seemed carved from stone, yet his eyes blazed.

'I am the voice of Aggedor,' came Hepesh's chilly tones. 'I am his eyes, his ears, his messenger ! No one but I—'

Peladon cut in, harshly. 'Are you above the king? I am the king. You heard my words. They were addressed to my servant, Aggedor. You in turn are *his* servant, and *my* subject ! Do not argue with your king !'

It was as though Peladon had struck the old man in the face. Hepesh seemed to flinch, then, drawing in his anger, he composed his face, and bowed before speaking. 'All is ready at the Pit of Combat, majesty. We only await only your presence.'

.        .        .        .        .

Reluctantly, Alpha Centauri and Arcturus had agreed to attend the deadly contest—but not without protest. 'Our presence is not required,' insisted Arcturus. 'We must make ourselves ready to escape, if necessary !'

'I cannot face such a barbaric ceremony,' shrilled Alpha Centauri. 'I shall faint—I know it !'

Izlyr would make no allowances. 'It is essential that the Commission be present,' he hissed, 'if we are to make an adequate and objective report to the Galactic Council.' This was something that the other delegates couldn't very well argue with, and, silently, they took their places. Jo deliberately placed herself near Izlyr and Ssorg. Whatever the Doctor thought of them, Jo thought they were the only people to be trusted. The only people now missing were the king and Hepesh. The king's chair was set within an enclosed cubicle at a prime viewing point along the gallery that encircled the upper rim of the Pit of Combat. He would sit down alone. All other observers were free to move about the gallery, and watch from whatever vantage point they chose.

'He may yet survive,' whispered Izlyr to Jo.

Her face was drawn, and she shook her head wanly. 'You haven't seen Grun in his armour, Izlyr. I have. He's —' she paused, trying not to sound utterly defeatist, 'he's going to be very hard to beat.' Her voice trailed away. Into the royal box stepped Peladon. The combat would soon begin.

Everyone was nervously awaiting the arrival of Grun and the Doctor. Jo looked down into the Pit. She had half expected an arena rather like a Roman ampitheatre; flat, sandy, with steep walls and a cage-like entrance. The Pit was very different. The entrance was covered by a heavily spiked portcullis. The floor was of highly polished granite so smooth that it reflected like a lake of still water. There were only three small areas in which direct combat could easily take place. All the rest of the ground space was filled with steps, mounds, steep slopes and a jumbled medley of pillars and short columns of stone. On the walls, on the pillars, and scattered here and there about the Pit, were a variety of weapons : a four-edged axe, a sword with a broad blade that became a vicious prong, a lance with a barbed, three-forked head, and a triple ball and chain, hideously spiked. She shuddered, and was about to turn away when the portcullis slowly opened—and into that strange arena, stepped Grun and the Doctor.

The formalities were simple. The two combatants were to march to the centre of the arena, turn and face the king, and await his signal. They could take up or reject any weapon, choosing those that would best deal with whatever situation arose. No tactic was forbidden. From the moment the contest started, the only aim was to kill. Surrender was not allowed. One man only must leave the Pit alive.

Side by side, the strangely matched pair walked to the

centre of the arena and paused. The Doctor, flamboyant and unprotected, looked up and saw the distant figure of Jo, high above. He gave a small, confident wave, and smiled. Grun, too, saw the Earth Princess, and her words echoed inside his head—only to be drowned by the final words of the High Priest.

'He is our enemy, Grun,' Hepesh repeated fiercely. 'For the honour of the king and of Aggedor, he must be destroyed. Do your duty—kill!' He struggled to concentrate on the task in hand, and nearly overstepped the centre marker. The Doctor's cheerful voice murmured in his ear, irritatingly bland. 'Watch what you're doing, Grun old chap. You'll spoil the show otherwise.'

As the king stood up, they bowed in unison. They rose, and looked up at his slight but regal figure, poised above them. He raised a hand. In it he held a scarlet pennant, bright against the drab grey of the castle stones. The fluttering scarlet fell. The fight had begun.

Neither of them had been inside the Pit before, but Grun had at least viewed it many times from the gallery above. He studied its complexities and hidden snags, and knew the dangers of the polished stones. More than this, none of the deadly weapons in the Pit were strange to him. Some were so antique that they were no longer used—but he, as the King's Champion, had had access to them and had taken delight in testing their power. Other weapons were more common and, thus, he was even more skilled in their use. His rich armour weighed on him, but this was necessary. With the correct arms, he was impregnable. While he loped towards the weapons that he wanted, the Doctor scarcely moved. The alien was obviously confused by his surroundings. Now was the moment to strike and strike swiftly, for there was no honour in baiting a helpless opponent. His hand grasped the razor-edged flail, and the nearby shield : he stood, immense and magnificent— and all thought of mercy left his mind. He was the greatest of Peladon's warriors, and it was a warrior's destiny to kill.

Although apparently still and unmoving, the Doctor

had swiftly taken in the bizarre contrasts of the Pit. He had also seen Grun move, none too swiftly, to pick up a weapon that he obviously knew was there. It was now the Doctor's turn to find some means of defending himself before Grun attacked. But from where he was standing, he could see no suitable weapon. Grun was almost on top of him before the Doctor slipped nimbly to one side and began to clamber up a short slope. The flail slashed down, missing the Doctor by inches. He looked back and saw the marks where the razor-sharp blades had scoured the stone, and blinked: this was no time for the finer points of ring technique! He scrambled rapidly out of Grun's range, and looked about him desperately for a weapon. A bright hilt glinted close by, and he grabbed at it eagerly—then almost immediately flung it from him. It had been a poignard, little more than eighteen inches long and no defence at all against the vicious blades that Grun used so deftly. Again, the flail sang its deadly song through the air; again the Doctor dodged, this time nearly slipping from his higher vantage point, down to the smooth granite below. He altered his balance in mid-air and swung away from Grun's next sweeping blow. He grasped a nearby hanging net. It was made of finely wrought metal, and linked so ingeniously as to be as supple as fine cord. Yet, in itself, it wasn't simply defensive: every link thrust out a wickedly pointed hook.

The Doctor lifted the net from the wall, and stood poised several feet above Grun. The Doctor realised that he had, for once, a definite advantage: his positioning was good and Grun knew the dangers presented by that clawing net! If he could only cast it skilfully enough . . . The net flew through the air. Grun, neatly side-stepping, avoided its tearing barbs. Even so, he slipped and found his flail caught and tangled in the metal net. One jerk from the Doctor, and the weapon was torn from Grun's gauntleted hand. But its weight made the net useless, and both men ran for other weapons. The Doctor took up a trident-headed spear. Grun now held a massive, four-bladed axe. The spear was not balanced for throwing, but could keep Grun at bay long enough for the Doctor to size up his next move—or so the Doctor thought. With surprising agility, Grun shifted his position to a stump of stone overlooking the Doctor, and swung the axe at the full limit of its shaft. The Doctor barely had time to turn and clumsily parry the blow. His spearshaft was reduced to a useless stump in his hands. With a roar, Grun struck out again, leaping downwards at the Doctor as the axe heads glinted in the torchlight. Nimbly, the Doctor leaped to one side, but miscalculated his footing, stumbled, and fell sprawling on the smooth granite below. In a flash, Grun had sprung after him, and stood poised, arms high, the axe at its peak—but before it could be brought flashing down to cleave its target, the Doctor, at full-length, flicked out a stabbing foot against Grun's left ankle. Grun toppled and fell, like a mighty tree. Unable to take advantage of Grun's position, the Doctor rolled aside and sought yet another means of defending himself. Grun, in turn, found the axe shaft had shattered on impact with the granite floor, and he too sought another weapon—this time, the fearsome triple ball, spiked and spinning from its shafted chain. He reared up to his full height, and began to whirl the chains about his head. Instantly, the Doctor recognised them as a variation on the South American bolas. Thrown through the air, they could bring down a charging bull; or tear a man to shreds. As Grun hesitated, the Doctor seized a two pronged throwing spear and flung it, full-force. His aim was sure. The prongs caught Grun's throwing arm at its full stretch upward and he was yanked backwards, his arm pinned against the stone by the prongs of the spear. The throwing chains, entwined around the prongs and shaft of the Doctor's spear, made it impossible to shake free, even though Grun's great strength tore the prongs from the wall behind him. His effort brought him stumbling down the incline to the arena below, and it was here that the Doctor took his chance. From a ledge at the height of Grun's shoulder, the Doctor gave a sharp, explosive cry, and launched himself into a flying jump-kick. The impact of his out-

*The Doctor launched himself into a flying jump-kick*

thrust heels caught the already staggering Grun on the side of the neck, close to his Adam's apple—and the effect was spectacular and horrifying. As Grun smashed into the dust, his helmet went flying. He began to fight desperately for breath, his great gauntlets tearing at his throat, his lungs pumping and rasping as he tried to suck in precious air. His bulging eyes hardly saw the Doctor take up the poignard that he had once thrown down as useless. With Grun lying helpless, it was the perfect weapon for the *coup de grâce*. The Doctor knelt over the fallen King's Champion and, with deliberate precision, placed the needle-sharp point against his opponent's neck. Grun, still heaving for breath, grew still. His staring eyes fixed on the Doctor's face. He knew he was as good as dead—but still he gave no indication of fear.

In the gallery above, all eyes were fixed on the scene in the Pit. Peladon, standing, made no sound. Raising his eyes, he found Jo staring at him from across the open space. And in that split second, her gaze went past the king, first to Hepesh, slinking away into the shadows, and then to a more threatening form, its menace concentrated on the Doctor in the arena below—and Jo screamed.

The Doctor did not hear that scream. He was offering Grun his hand. 'Live, Grun . . .' he said quietly. 'I will not kill the King's Champion.'

Grun, his face gaping with amazement, let himself be hauled up. And it was at that moment that the Doctor heard Izlyr's harsh warning. When he looked up, the warlord's face was turned to Ssorg, and his grim, gloved hand was pointing across the length of the Pit.

'Doctor!' came the explosive whisper, then 'Ssorg—kill!'

In the same split second that Jo screamed again, Grun flung the Doctor to the ground. The ground on which he had been standing exploded into white heat as the laser beam from Arcturus's gun seared into action. But it was the last shot that Arcturus ever fired. Ssorg's sonic destructor, ordered into action by Izlyr, fired also—and it was the sight of Arcturus's destruction that brought the scream of horror to Jo's throat. Under the impact of the intense sonic pulse, the shape of the neuroplasm first distorted, horribly, then vanished in a burst of particles. Jo, turning away from the dreadful sight, could only gasp what she and the others all about her at last knew: the secret enemy of Peladon and the evil force behind Hepesh was delegate Arcturus.

# 9

# A Conspiracy of Terror

Hepesh had lingered only long enough to see the swift destruction of his alien ally. While the confusion over Arcturus's clumsy attack on the Doctor still raged, the High Priest took what he knew would be his only chance of escape. With the Doctor alive, and the link between Hepesh and the alien explained, nothing remained but to fall back on the plan that had lurked in his mind long before Arcturus had suggested the sharing of power . . . This defeat, and what he had heard from the king's own mouth in the temple before the ritual combat, convinced Hepesh that the last resort—a palace revolution—was inevitable. The plans had been prepared; armed men that he could count on were at hand. What he would tell those who were loyal to the old ways, to the spirit of Aggedor, would send them swiftly against these arrogant aliens and even against the king himself. It was enough to claim that the young king was possessed, invaded by the alien evil. Once Hepesh became regent once more, that evil would be forever purged. The Federation would be only too glad to rid itself of such a source of trouble. The delegates would return to their planets and peace would reign on Peladon once more—with, or without its present king. Hepesh had ruled with honour before, and he could do so again. But this time, it would be on *his* terms!

III

In the throne room, celebration mingled with sadness. The revelation of Hepesh's strange ally had profoundly distressed Peladon. To have Hepesh disagree with him was almost natural, given the difference in their age and outlook. But to find himself betrayed by a man he had trusted all his life . . . Not even the quiet wisdom of the Doctor could heal that wound.

'There was no malice towards you, your majesty,' the Doctor murmured, 'only a fanatical love of the past.'

'And a corresponding hatred of the future,' whispered Izlyr. 'He would stop at nothing to prevent the Federation gaining a foothold here.'

'It is almost inconceivable . . .' wailed Alpha Centauri, 'that a Federation delegate should be involved in subversive activities of such a violent nature ! I would have trusted Arcturus with my life.'

'That would have been most unwise,' hissed Izlyr.

'But the attack on Arcturus,' wondered Jo, 'it nearly killed him.'

'Faked,' said the Doctor. 'He simply told Hepesh what to do to make it look as though he had been the victim of an assassination plot.'

Izlyr nodded. 'As I suspected. But there was no proof.'

'What about the things I found on the balcony, and in Izlyr's room ?' queried Jo.

'Planted by Hepesh, Jo,' replied the Doctor, 'to stir up suspicion amongst the delegates themselves. If you hadn't discovered them, someone would have.'

'But the manifestation of Aggedor—' interrupted Peladon.

'That wasn't easy, your majesty,' said the Doctor. 'You must've noticed yourself, it didn't happen every time . . .'

'The Royal Beast didn't appear when that huge statue fell,' trilled Alpha Centauri, 'nor when Arcturus was attacked.'

'It must've taken a fair bit of handling, that's why,' retorted the Doctor. 'You see, the sacred beast is not extinct. Hepesh found that a few still existed on the far slopes of Mount Megeshra, the holy mountain. He managed to capture one—heaven alone knows how—kept it hidden in a sort of lair beneath the citadel, and trained it to do his bidding in some way.'

'He made the Royal Beast . . . perform? Like a circus animal? But how?' demanded the king.

'There are various ways,' murmured the Doctor, his face serious. 'Kindness, conditioning by a system of rewards—and cruelty. The last one's the most likely, I'm afraid. Hepesh had to act quickly and effectively, and it was necessary to have the beast in a permanent state of fury.' He paused. 'In fact, Aggedor is a highly intelligent animal who would respond willingly to gentle persuasion —given the chance.'

Peladon said nothing. His mind brooded on the man who had once had a hand in educating him in kingly responsibilities. Was power so important that Hepesh should degrade himself to the level of a common assassin—and, in the process, treat the Royal Beast as though it were a common cur, yet all the time revering its holy image as all-powerful?

'But why did he do all this?' demanded Jo. 'What could he hope to gain? He was already the second most important person, next to the king.'

'He had to have complete control of the planet and its resources,' said the Doctor. 'And that's where Arcturus came in.'

'After all he had said,' muttered the king. 'Then to have allied himself with an alien that he claimed to despise . . .'

'I still don't understand what Arcturus was after,' said Jo, looking puzzled.

It was Izlyr that answered her. 'Peladon is rich in mineral deposits. The planet of Arcturus is within ten years of running out of its own natural resources. That's why Arcturus had to make sure Peladon didn't become part of the Galactic Federation. He could then make an independent treaty with Hepesh, take all the minerals required, and leave the Pel economy apparently unchanged. It was a neat trick. Virtually nothing would be paid and

Peladon would be even more backward. In fact, exploitation of the worst kind!'

'Extremely unethical!' squealed Alpha Centauri. 'Fortunately the scheme has been foiled and all is well!'

'I'm not so sure about that,' said the Doctor grimly.

'But Arcturus is dead!' exclaimed Jo.

'Yes, but Hepesh is very much alive and kicking,' insisted the Doctor. 'It was Arcturus who sold Hepesh on the idea that joining the Federation would mean slavery. Now, nothing will ever change that belief. Hepesh will go to any lengths to prevent this planet losing its independence. And I don't just mean civil war!'

'Such violent action would conflict directly with the peaceful intentions of the Federation!' twittered Alpha Centauri, palpitating with shock. 'We will be forced to disengage ourselves from further negotiations!'

'That may be more difficult than you think, Alpha old chap,' declared the Doctor. 'Hepesh could cause an awful lot of trouble at Federation level, if he wanted to.'

'There will be no more attempts to harm delegates,' Peladon said firmly. 'My royal guard will see to that.'

'We can defend ourselves,' whispered the Martian warlord, 'if the situation calls for such extreme measures.'

'Hepesh knows he can't compete against the power of your weapons,' pointed out the Doctor. 'He'd be cleverer than that. For instance, he could accuse Izlyr and Ssorg of murdering Arcturus over a political dispute. Even though it isn't true, can you imagine the consequences?'

'Yes,' hissed Izlyr, 'Mars and the world of Arcturus are old enemies. There would be war!'

'Exactly,' agreed the Doctor. 'Within no time at all, the rest of the Federation would be taking sides, and then—'

'The Federation would be wrecked!' cried Alpha Centauri. 'It would mean a vast, interplanetary conflict; a terrible war, using the most destructive weapons!'

The Doctor turned a sombre face to Peladon, and directed his words to the young king. 'And Peladon will be the first battlefield—blasted, sterile, and forgotten . . .'

Peladon had heard tales of what alien weapons could do. There was no escape from the invisible clouds that brought disease or radiation sickness. It would be not merely the land and the buildings standing upon it which would be destroyed by the first fire-blasts. In time, the people too—those who escaped the initial destruction—would be swept away utterly by the sickness of the bone, or a plague to end all plagues. There would be no more children and no more beasts born. No seeds would ever grow to fruit again. The planet would become first sterile, then a living tomb, then as cold and barren as the three moons that circle Peladon. In the end, Hepesh would have won nothing but death. But to him, even this would be better than enslavement by the aliens. The old man must be blind not to see that, in time to come, the aliens would return—to tear the heart out of the dead planet. And not a soul would be alive to prevent it.

Peladon looked at the Doctor with haunted eyes. His voice was low. 'Tell me . . . what should I do?'

'You must remove Hepesh from office by a royal decree and replace him with someone you can trust.' Izlyr nodded in agreement.

Peladon brooded. 'The shame will destroy him.'

'It isn't easy being a king, your majesty,' observed the Doctor sympathetically. 'But unless you remove Hepesh, everything you have worked for will be ruined. You must choose . . . now!'

Peladon had to think rapidly. Jo watched him, and knew something of what he felt. Hepesh, enemy though he might now be, had once been a dear friend. If Peladon chose to withdraw, he would forfeit any hope of future Federation help. If he decided to go ahead with negotiations, he would have to eliminate the destructive influence of Hepesh. Either way, the loss to his planet would be immense. Which would he take? All eyes were on the frowning face of the young king. Only the Doctor let his gaze be caught by a nearly imperceptible gesture from Grun. The Doctor questioned the hovering form of the King's Champion with a silent glance. The reply came in a subtle series of mimed gestures. And before he had the chance to deduce what Grun was trying to communicate the king was speaking again. Before the youth on the throne had finished, Grun had slipped away, unnoticed

'If there should be civil war,' asked Peledon, sharp eyed,' will I receive the full backing of the Federation?'

The Doctor and Izlyr were about to give their consent —but it was the desperately anxious voice of Alpha Cen tauri that answered the king. 'The Federation charter does not permit our involvement in internal politics.'

Izlyr turned on Alpha Centauri, his voice and gaze stern. 'A unanimous decision can summon emergency powers and, if necessary, call on our orbiting space craft for technical assistance!'

'It would be a break with all precedent!' protested Alpha Cenauri.

Jo remonstrated. 'Alpha Centauri, the circumstances are unique! And your own safety is involved, don't for get.'

The hexapod was adamant. 'I can't persuade myself that interference of this kind is legally justified.' The shrill voice trailed away to a plaintive squawk as the hexapod swung its great and lustrous eye from Izlyr back to Ssorg They were advancing upon Alpha Centauri in a most threatening fashion!

'There are principles involved . . ,' the squeaking voice tried to sound majestic and determined. Instead, Jo thought, it sounded more like a squeezy doll.

'Principles, eh?' smiled the Doctor, with a nod to Izlyr and Ssorg. 'A private conference should settle those . . .' As Ssorg and Izlyr closed in on Alpha Centauri, and firmly but politely escorted the hexapod out of the throne room the Doctor turned to Peladon, and bowed. 'Will you ex cuse us, your majesty,' he said drily, 'while we reach a unanimous decision . . . in private . . .'

Peladon stood, his head proud and erect, a slight smile on his lips. 'Give me that reassurance, Doctor—and I shall act without hesitation!'

Where once before he had been a civic dignitary, richly clothed for the king's court, Hepesh now wore light armour beneath his cloak of temple rank. The captains he had summoned to him knew what that meant; when a priest of the temple took up arms, it was at the command of Aggedor, to preserve the kingdom! Hepesh had many months earlier, selected wisely. With long experience of diplomacy, his instinctive distrust of the aliens had warned him to be prepared for any emergency—even civil war. He was not such a fool as to waste time explaining to those loyal followers the petty details of their situation. It was enough to say that their nation was at risk, their freedom about to be violated, and their king charmed by the trickery of the aliens. Aggedor could see the truth, and had pointed the way to victory. The aliens must go.

With the death of Arcturus, there was no hiding Hepesh's intentions from the Assessment Committee—and this in itself, might bring a bloodless victory, should the aliens decide to withdraw from the planet. That would surely happen if the wriggling squid Alpha Centauri got its own way. Then, Peladon would be left to its own barbaric ways and there would be no more alien interference. But until their spaceships slipped out of orbit and back into their starpaths home, there would be danger. The temple of Aggedor within the citadel was no refuge. Instead, Hepesh would muster his forces in the catacombs beneath the castle and the ancient shrine there. It was small, but holy, and in it was stored all the extra weapons that his personal military elite would need. Superb soldiers, sworn only to the service of Aggedor, they would be more than a match for the king's Royal Guard. But first they must be gathered, and the final details given to them. By moonrise, if the aliens had not left, the avengers of Aggedor would strike.

One by one, the captains came to him. They reported their weapon strength and position within the catacombs. Even as they came, certain tasks were being carried out. There was, however, but one rule that Hepesh hammered home relentlessly.

'Contact with the aliens must be avoided at all cost,' he ordered, 'for they have weapons that could destroy us in a moment. When the time comes, it is I who will face them, alone and unarmed.'

This strategy sounded madness to his men—until he explained the reasoning behind it. For the plan Hepesh had formed was utterly simple. There would be no skirmishes with the aliens and no attempts to take the whole citadel by force. There was only one target: to take the throne room and hold the king hostage.

⁂

Grun, too, was thinking on simple and direct lines. He was a warrior, and he had a score to settle. Faithful to both his king and to Aggedor, he had been betrayed into a false loyalty. The strange alien who fought without armour, yet who in victory had spared Grun's life, had shown the truth. Hepesh the patriot was a low hypocrite who had worked with an alien enemy to bring about the downfall of the king. The alien, Arcturus, was dead. Now it was the turn of Hepesh. With that source of evil dead or captured, there could be no revolt. It was a matter of finding him, and Grun knew where he would go. Deep in the catacombs, there was a shrine. Grun, when he had prepared to become King's Champion, had kept his vigil there. It was said to be the most holy place upon the whole of Mount Megeshra. It was a place that few men knew of, and where even fewer would dare to go. Since that vigil long ago, Grun had never returned there. But now, his purpose was greater than his fear: Hepesh would be there, and Hepesh must be taken.

Grun's long stride took him swiftly along the shadowed corridor to the alcove that he knew so well. Pulling aside the tapestry, a twist of the torch holder opened the way into the tunnel beyond. But for once, Grun was not careful to hide his route. He tied the tapestry back, a sure signal for those who had eyes to see that someone had gone before. He entered, and the stone door closed after him. Once inside the tunnel, the roughness of the slabbed loor and the relatively cramped space of his surroundings orced him to move more carefully. In spite of his burly rame, however, he moved almost silently. Soon he was it the limit of the torchlight, and moving into the phosphor-dim darkness beyond. He needed no map, and he vas careful to skirt those tunnels that led to the temple of Aggedor, and to those deeper paths that were the Royal Beast's special domain. Only the very brave, the mad, or ritual victims took that way. And Grun would let nothing leter him from his target : Hepesh.

* * * * *

Alpha Centauri could hardly object to having an escort vhen, after all, they were fellow delegates. Nevertheless, he hexapod could not dispel a distinct feeling of unease at he forcible speed with which he was being taken to the lelegates' conference room.

'Do not forget, delegate Izlyr,' complained Alpha Centauri, 'that I have the right to veto any suggestions that are against the Federation's better interests!'

'You will have that oportunity, I assure you,' hissed the Martian warlord. 'But you will probably think twice before using it.'

Alpha Centauri swivelled its head in an attempt to see just how far behind were the Doctor and the Princess. Too far to hear Izlyr's suspiciously menacing remark, the hexapod noticed with a shudder. The Martian was not an easy person to get on with. It might be better to humour him a little, perhaps even to hint at concessions.

'It would be different if there were precedents for such a situation,' trilled the nervous hexapod, 'but there are not. We must consider all our options. We must not act rashly!'

'I am convinced of the value of reason,' whispered Izlyr sardonically, 'and I am sure you will see the matter *our* way ... eventually.'

'Well of course,' squeaked Alpha Centauri, trying to be cheerful, 'I'm perfectly willing to listen to *reason* ...'

'Good,' coughed the Martian. 'That will save us all a great deal of trouble.'

A considerable way behind the delegates came the Doctor and Jo. She was still inclined to believe that Hepesh on his own represented little or no real threat to the work of the delegates' committee, or the king's choice.

'Jo,' insisted the Doctor patiently, 'you really must take Hepesh seriously! Given the chance, he could still bring Peladon round to his way of thinking—if only to save the population of this planet from being wiped out!'

'But if that was to happen,' Jo mused, 'Hepesh would have won . . . without a fight.'

'Exactly! And Peladon will have lost!' snapped the Doctor. 'I tell you, Hepesh will try anything!'

'Well, he can't accuse Izlyr of murder—there were witnesses,' stated Jo firmly. 'You and me, for a start—we saw what happened. Izlyr saved your life!'

The Doctor looked at her and smiled wryly. 'You're forgetting something Jo, aren't you? Officially, we don't exist. We're nothing but a pair of impostors!'

Jo stopped, and pulled the Doctor to a halt. She glared angrily up into his surprised face. 'Look—he didn't save your life just because you're supposed to be the grand Chairman Delegate! It was you as a person!'

'And supposing the real Earth Delegate arrives?' demanded the Doctor. 'Who's going to accept my word then?'

Jo's anger at what she saw as the Doctor's vanity boiled over. But even as she spoke, he was looking past her towards the alcove nearby—which only added to her feelings of irritation. 'Honestly! What with you playing the Grand Ambassador, Alpha Centauri upstaging every one with those ridiculous tentacles, and Peladon acting like a wet fish—someone ought to take the lot of you and bang your heads together!' She paused for breath. 'You're not even listening!'

'So that's what Grun was trying to say!' exclaimed the Doctor furiously.

'What are you talking about?' asked Jo, trying to see

what it was that the Doctor was so interested in. There wasn't anything—just an empty alcove and a rotten old tapestry, all rumpled up.

Taking her by the elbow, the Doctor urged her after Izlyr and Ssorg. 'Now, Jo . . . you go ahead. Help Izlyr to work on old Alpha Cenauri . . .' He gave her one of his most charming smiles and, with a small shove, propelled her along the corridor away from him. 'Once you've got the chap on our side, tell Peladon!'

Half-heartedly, Jo moved after the three aliens, who were now well ahead. She looked to see where they'd got to, speaking to the Doctor as she looked away from him.

'But I don't understand. What are you going to do?'

'I'm going to see a man about a door,' came the reply. But when she turned to ask him what he meant by such a idiotic remark, the Doctor had vanished.

    .     .     .     .     .

The last details of Hepesh's plan were being spelled out to the leader of the crack unit that Hepesh had specially selected for the most difficult task : the taking of the king.

'My men are armed and ready, my Lord Hepesh,' reported the tense-faced captain. Neither he nor Hepesh saw the burly shadow of Grun slip into the deeper darkness of the shrine and hide there, listening.

'Thank you, captain,' acknowledged the High Priest. 'Understand that no harm must come to the king. He is to be taken prisoner with as little force as necessary.'

'Yes, my lord,' replied the captain. 'But his personal bodyguard?'

'You need show no mercy towards them. They will not regard you or your men as friends . . .'

The captain smiled, his face cruel. 'My men fight to kill, my lord. They are the best.'

In the shadows, Grun's face tightened in cold anger. Once, every soldier had been the king's man, totally dedicated to his cause and comrade to every soldier. This man Hepesh had turned them against each other as though they were each other's enemies!

'Now, Captain,' continued Hepesh, 'at the moment we storm the throne room, two men must ignore the fighting and move immediately to seize the king. They must be—'

The High Priest stopped in mid-speech as Grun's mighty form stepped forward from the shadows. At first the captain and Hepesh, elated with the imminent success of their plan, assumed Grun to be at one with them. The sharp grate of his sword being drawn from its scabbard soon told them otherwise.

'Grun,' Hepesh exclaimed, extending his ringed hand in greeting, 'you have chosen well! I shall not—'

It was then he saw the glint of the naked sword, and knew that he was closer to death than he had ever before been. The captain stood between Hepesh and Grun and spun about at Hepesh's cry of warning, his sword at the ready.

'Captain—look out!'

The captain, like all soldiers in the citadel, knew Grun to be the greatest of the king's warriors, but he was no coward. With a swift lunge, he attacked. Over the ring of blade on blade, it was the High Priest's voice that called: 'Guards! To me!'

The captain, brave as he was, stood little chance against Grun's strength and skill. With a sweeping, backhanded stroke, the King's Champion severed the tendons of the captain's sword arm. Before the sword had fallen to the ground, the follow-up lunge to the throat had ended the captain's life. Grun turned to find the enemy that he had come for—but Hepesh knew Grun's intent, and had slipped into the shadows by the door. Before Grun could locate him, the sound of armed men behind him made Grun turn. Facing him were two more of Hepesh's picked commandos. At the sight of Grun, they faltered—but had no other choice but to fight for their lives. Handling two opponents with arrogant ease, Grun brought one down with a straight-armed stab to the chest—that very move, however, left him blind to the figure of Hepesh, who, coming in behind him, struck the great warrior on his unprotected head with a massive stone from the altar footing. Without a sound, Grun toppled to the ground, and lay there utterly still. Without glancing at the fallen body, Hepesh stepped over Grun, and moved out to the tunnel. 'Come!' he called to the waiting commandos. 'It is time! The hour of Aggedor is at hand.'

## 10

## The Battle for the Palace

Jo looked at the alien delegates impatiently. Splitting hairs was getting them nowhere. 'This discussion's gone on long enough,' she said. 'What about taking a vote?'

Alpha Cenauri immediately raised several tentacles in protest. This was normal procedure on intergalactic civil service committees. A decision too quickly arrived at aroused suspicion. A certain degree of niggling was needed to give respectability to the motion under discussion.

'I object!' shrilled the hexapod formally. But before the objection could be elaborated, Jo turned on Alpha Cenauri with a frown of irritation.

'And I object to your stupid objections!' she snapped. 'You've done nothing but split hairs and raise points of order since we started!'

'Point of order! The speaker is not an official member of this committee.'

'Whose side are you on?' exclaimed Jo. 'While you're babbling away, people could be getting killed!'

'Decisions can only be arrived at by properly performed democratic methods,' insisted Alpha Centauri. 'If you would care to inspect the appropriate book of rules—'

'Will you make up your mind!' shouted Jo.

There was a short silence. Alpha Centauri turned a delicate shade of blue, and gave a slow blink of its single watery eye. It didn't like being shouted at.

'The motion has to be put in the proper manner,' piped

Alpha Centauri plaintively. 'Anger isn't at all necessary.

'The motion is that this Committee of Assessment urge the Federation to support King Peladon in every wa possible in bringing peace to this troubled planet,' hisse the Martian warlord. 'Those in favour?'

Both he and Ssorg raised their fists—at the same tim looking at their quivering and reluctant colleague. Unde their grim gaze, a frail blue tentacle wavered upwards

'Carried unanimously,' whispered Izlyr, triumphantly

'Thank goodness for that,' said Jo, adding hastily, 'A very wise decision, Alpha Centauri. Well done!'

'I trust so, Princess,' came the miserable reply. 'But, fo the record, my agreement is registered under protest. accept no responsibility!'

'Protest noted,' observed Izlyr. 'The next step is to in form the Federation and request immediate technica assistance. Perhaps, Alpha Centauri, as senior civil ser vant—'

'My apologies,' twittered the hexapod, 'but that wil not be possible.'

Izlyr rose to his feet. The impassiveness of his warrio mask, although showing no feelings, made him appea coldly threatening. Alpha Centauri flinched involun tarily. 'Are you refusing to put into operation a decisio arrived at without dissent?' the Martian demanded.

The hexapod, under the gaze of its three angry com panions, flushed and flowed through several shades o blue into green and back again before giving its haltin answer. 'It isn't like that at all. My reason is technical, no personal. My surface-to-spaceship communicator is no functioning. I can do nothing with it . . .'

'That sounds like a coward's excuse,' hissed Izlyr.

'I protest—I mean, it is nothing of the sort,' cried Alpha Centauri. 'I am not a technically trained operator. I d not know the cause, but there is obviously a serious mal function.'

'Then we will use our own system,' whispered Izlyr. 'I is without doubt technically superior to yours. And whil Ssorg makes contact with our spacecraft, I will personall inspect this communicator.' The warlord moved to the door, and added darkly. 'We do not want a repeat of the trick that incapacitated Arcturus . . .'

Jo watched the two Martians leave. She then turned back to Alpha Centauri and frowned. 'Why didn't you mention that you'd lost contact with your ship? It might've been important.'

'I have had no reason to make a report until the combat ceremony,' replied Alpha Centauri. 'Since then, so many things have happened, I gave no thought to the matter. In fact, I feel totally confused!'

They were suddenly aware that Ssorg was standing in the doorway. He said nothing—but in his hands was a compact piece of apparatus. It was hopelessly smashed.

'What has happened!' exclaimed Alpha Centauri, flustering its way towards Ssorg. Almost immediately, Izlyr entered and seeing the broken unit in Ssorg's hands, whirled to face the others.

'Sabotage!' he whispered fiercely. 'Our own communicator has been destroyed—and yours, Alpha Centauri, failed because it was deliberately tampered with!'

'Then we're completely cut off!' cried Jo. As the others looked at her she explained quickly, 'Our own unit was badly damaged when we crashed.'

'Without our communicators, we cannot return to our spacecraft!' wailed Alpha Centauri.

Izlyr turned to Jo. 'Princess, is there no other way that you or the Doctor can communicate with your spaceship?'

'Spaceship . . .' repeated Jo, blankly, then realised that unlike Izlyr and Alpha Centauri, there wasn't an Earth spaceship orbiting the planet in wait for her and the Doctor!

'Er . . . no—I'm afraid there isn't,' she said quickly, then hastily clarified the statement. 'I mean there isn't another way of making contact.'

'That is a pity,' hissed Izlyr. 'Particularly in view of the special arrangements that will undoubtedly have to be made.'

Jo looked at the Martian, her face puzzled. 'I don't quite understand,' she said. 'What arrangements?'

'For your forthcoming wedding to King Peladon,' answered Izlyr. 'Admit that is the purpose of your visit.'

The burst of laughter that followed Jo's first look of alarm took the three aliens by surprise. Surely a royal engagement was a dignified matter?

'I'm sorry to disappoint you,' bubbled Jo, controlling her fit of giggles with difficulty, 'but a marriage has *not* been arranged. To coin a phrase, we're just good friends . . . hardly that, even.'

'But it would have made a splendid climax to the king's coronation!' cried Alpha Centauri.

'Well, you can forget it,' exclaimed Jo. 'And anyway, before we have a coronation, we have to have a king. *Are* you going to help Peladon or not?'

'Without contact with our spacecraft, we are trapped,' observed Izlyr. 'We can hardly take the offensive with only three operative agents.' He threw a brief look at the quivering hexapod, and explained, 'I do not include you, Alpha Centauri. You are a natural pacifist, and your habitual hysteria will do nothing for our morale.'

'Two,' corrected Ssorg. 'The Doctor is not with us, Lord Izlyr.'

'We need him. Where is he?' demanded the warlord, turning to Jo. 'He must be told that we are trapped!'

'I don't know where he is. I think he was going to find Grun . . . but he didn't tell me why.'

Alpha Centauri was becoming agitated again.

'There's no escape!' the hexapod cried, 'And now, the Doctor has vanished. I knew something like this would happen!'

Jo spoke to the jittery alien firmly but kindly. 'Centauri, stop it at once. Nothing has happened yet. We're perfectly safe here in the citadel—and they won't dare attack Federation delegates.'

'But these people are barbarians!' shrilled the deep blue hexapod. 'And Hepesh *hates* us . . . we are at his mercy!'

A military situation was one which Izlyr could understand instinctively, and he spoke with cold precision. 'As hostages, we would be of great value to Hepesh.'

'That'd just about finish everything!' exclaimed Jo.

'Agreed,' nodded Izlyr. 'We must take suitable precautions. Let us hope we do not have to put them into operation.'

   .    &    .    .    .

The Royal Guards, like Grun, were hand-picked for their total loyalty to the king, and the excellence of their strength and ability as warriors. Their regimental motif, identical on helmet, breastplate, and the proud pennants that they paraded on ceremonial occasions, was the head of Aggedor in profile surmounted by a crown. Their motto read : the king above all. Traitors would be granted no mercy. But the last persons they expected to see disloyal to the king were Hepesh and the Commander of the Temple Guard. Rumours were flying thick and fast around the barrack room, but no one had yet thought fit to confirm that Hepesh was the declared enemy of the king. Peladon himself had held this order of the day back until he knew for certain where he stood with the Federation. Until they were told otherwise, the Royal Guard accepted Hepesh as High Priest and Chancellor; out of favour, perhaps, but still officially in power. That trust was soon to be bitterly betrayed.

Hepesh's knowledge of the secret ways of the citadel was of the greatest value to his swift campaign. He had denied all knowledge of the secret tunnels to the king—because that knowledge was the key to the rebellion. Now, that key was being put to use. The tunnels beneath the citadel had gained them a silent access to the temple. From there, a select handful of men had made their way through the narrow passages which were set between the massive stone walls. Eventually, they had reached the balcony overlooking the main throne room doors, and there they waited for their rebellious lord, Hepesh, to make the next move. They hadn't long to wait. Hepesh and his guard commander aproached the throne room, pretending to be oblivious of the guards on duty there. Whatever it was they were discussing so seriously brought them to a halt. Hepesh bowed his head and seemed to listen intently to what his guard commander had to say. In fact, he was glancing furtively upwards to the balcony over the heads of the impassive Royal Guards. Yes, the commando scouts were there, ready and waiting. But, as he thought, the Royal Guards, half hidden as they were by the ledge of the balcony, were not an easy target. They would have to be brought forward for an attack to be properly effective. There must be no sounds of fighting before the throne room doors were open.

Hepesh solved the problem with typical directness. Turning from his guard commander, he called to the two Royal Guards. At his voice, they came to attention. In accordance with the customary method of addressing a person of high rank, they moved a full pace forward.

'You men—' called Hepesh, 'come here at once.'

The step forward that the Royal Guards took gave the commandos above the chance they needed. A short leap and they were on their prey, ruthlessly using their short swords to silence the guards for ever. The way to the throne room was now open and unguarded. But Hepesh waited. At his signal, the main group of attackers assembled on either side of the great doors. The next move involved hoisting the two handpicked men who were to deal with the king onto the balcony. There, they would make their way down to the concealed entrance inside the throne room. The moment the doors smashed open, and the inner guards were engaged by the oncoming commandos, these two infiltrators would dash straight past the main conflict to the king—and hold him at sword point. Hepesh would do the rest. All was ready. At the command of the High Priest, the massive doors were thrown open.

As the great doors burst open, Peladon rose to his feet in surprise and alarm. He had seen Hepesh, his temple cloak barely hiding the light armour beneath, and, all

*Peladon rose to his feet in surprise and alarm*

about him his personal temple guards, evil and menacing in their familar black helmets. His own Royal Guards reacted swiftly, forming a solid phalanx which blocked the way to the king. The fighting wedge formed by Hepesh's men was soon blunted, and they were soon reduced to desperate hand-to-hand skirmishes with the king's men. The king watched, amazed—yet with a touch of apprehension. For Grun was not with him, and Grun was the unconquerable defender of his royal master. The King's fear was soon justified. Racing towards him, outflanking the Royal Guards which so valiantly defended the entrance, came two black-helmeted figures. Unarmed, the king faced certain death. But the sword points thrust towards him halted at a hair's breadth from his throat. Turning his head, he called out: 'Hepesh—it is done! The king is ours!'

Until now, the king's men, a bare six in number, had more than held their own. In the confined space of the doorway, their trained movements, ruthlessly executed, had begun to drive the black helmets back. The cries of dying men and the clash of armour and swords, in turn almost drowned by the fierce shouts of the victorious Royal Guards, almost swamped Hepesh's clarion call. At first there was no pause, but he called again in a voice that had so often before proclaimed the message of Aggedor: 'Surrender—or your king will die!'

The second command had a greater effect, and the captain of the Royal Guard turned his head to check whether what Hepesh had said was true.

'Aggedor commands you. Throw down your arms, or the king dies!' The sword points pricked the king's throat. The eyes of the men standing at the king's side glowed with a fanatic intent. They would not hesitate to kill. There was no alternative for the Royal Guard but to obey—and it was the last command they ever heard. Hepesh had no intention of taking prisoners. The defenders' swords had scarcely left their hands before six bodies fell lifeless to the ground, struck down without mercy. Peladon flinched, closing his eyes to the brief slaughter. This was tradition at its most bloody. The fire in Hepesh's eyes promised little mercy even to Peladon himself. With a bold step, the High Priest strode to the throne, and there confronted his king and one-time ward. He paused there, and their eyes met.

'Is this the crown of kingship, Hepesh?' asked Peladon bravely, 'Or do you bring me death instead?'

Hepesh stared at the tense young face before him, and a distant memory returned to his mind: a boy whom he had once dandled on his knee, as a father might play with his son. But those days were past.

'You, Peladon, have become a stranger to the ways of Aggedor!' declaimed the haughty priest. 'You will be given the chance to return to our ancient ways, and in doing so you will live a glorious and revered figurehead of state.'

'Hepesh can never be king!' snapped Peladon.

'But as High Regent, I can guide this nation towards the destiny that it deserves!' retorted Hepesh. 'Deny that, deny Aggedor, and the royal line of Peladon is ended with the taking of your life!'

'The aliens will destroy you, Hepesh,' said the king calmly. 'You and all your people will be crushed in retribution. You cannot fight them and win . . .'

Hepesh smiled cruelly. He knew just how helpless the aliens were without their spaceships. His stealthy agents had seen to that. And there was still one more card that he would play against them.

'I am not a fool, Peladon,' he said. 'I do not intend to fight them and draw the vengeance of their fireships upon us. But they will listen to me. I have a weapon to which they have no answer.' He gestured brusquely. 'When I command, they will obey. And this nation will be free at last!'

.    .    .    .    .

The blow that had struck Grun down would have crushed the skull of a lesser man. But the same lunge that had left

Grun open to the blow from Hepesh had also pulled him out of its direct line of impact. Badly dazed, he was just beginning to come round when the Doctor arrived. Kneeling by the fallen King's Champion, and witnessing the dead bodies of the soldiers slain by Grun, the Doctor quickly put two and two together—and his face was grim.

'Grun, what's happened? Who do these soldiers belong to? Tell me!'

With an effort, the King's Champion pulled himself together, and focused on what the Doctor was asking him. His clumsy mime left the Doctor even more puzzled until Grun started scrawling an initial in the dust. As the letter 'H' was formed, the Doctor knew his suspicions were true. But if two soldiers were killed, how many more did Hepesh have with him? When asked, Grun put up his fingers again and again for the Doctor to count. The High Priest was moving too fast for the delegates to obtain sufficient help from Federation sources. Only direct action against Hepesh himself would do any good now.

'Its not good, Grun old chap. If Hepesh gains control of the citadel, I don't think we stand much chance.'

Grun grunted desperately and tried to make the Doctor understand that it wasn't the citadel that Hepesh hoped to take. He drew a circlet about his brow. Suddenly the Doctor understood. 'The king!' he exclaimed. 'Of course! Take the king and he's won everything!'

Grun lurched to his feet, grabbing up his fallen sword as he did so. He stood, swaying, a battered giant ready to take on Hepesh in a desperate attempt to save his king. The Doctor placed a hand on Grun's might arm, and shook his head. 'No, Grun, that isn't the way.'

His words were interrupted by a distant, echoing roar. Grun dropped to his knees and hid his face in the crook of his arm. He knew that cry: it was the Royal Beast, the mighty Aggedor!

'Its Aggedor . . .' murmured the Doctor, looking down the dark tunnel in the direction of the sound. That terrifying howl, far from striking terror into his heart, had given him an idea.

'Grun,' he said with a chuckle of delight, 'I think we may have a chance after all!'

The King's Champion looked at the mad alien in dumb amazement as the Doctor pulled him towards the eerie animal howl. Grun drew back. 'Come on, Grun,' coaxed the Doctor. 'You're not frightened, are you? You're the King's Champion, remember!'

Grun wasn't impressed with his own reputation—at least, not when it was a matter of confronting Aggedor. But the Doctor insisted. 'It's our only chance, Grun. And don't you worry—just leave everything to me.' Grun stared into the Doctor's eyes, uncertain. 'It's not for our sake, old chap, it's for the king,' said the Doctor firmly.

Grun took a deep breath, gripped his sword more tightly, and pointed the way ahead. The Doctor smiled. 'That's a good chap. I think you'll find that Aggedor will think on exactly the same lines as you do. Let's go and find out, shall we?'

.      .      .      .      .

When the knock on the delegates' room finally came, Izlyr and Ssorg were prepared. With Jo and Alpha Centauri safely out of the line of fire, the two Ice Warriors took up positions that commanded not only the door but the angle of the corridor outside that would be bound to contain the reinforcements. The door opened inward. Izlyr had worked out that against the primitive weapons of the Pels they could hold the room indefinitely. Food and water was a different matter. But if they could hold out for long enough, there was always the chance that the orbiting spacecraft would become suspicious and send down a scouting party. The knock came again, sharper, and with authority.

'Enter,' hissed the warlord, and prepared to fire.

There was only one man standing in the open doorway. It was Hepesh. He did not seem afraid.

'If you have men hidden outside, Ssorg will destroy you,' whispered Izlyr coldly. 'I warn you—do not attempt to harm us.'

'I am unarmed and alone,' retorted the High Priest.
'Where is the Doctor?'

'Somewhere you can't find him!' shouted Jo defiantly.

'He will not escape capture for long,' replied Hepesh,
arrogantly. 'The heart of the citadel is under my control.
You will all come with me to the throne room—now!'

'It's a trap!' shrilled Alpha Centauri, quivering in
alarm. 'He will kill all of us!'

'You will not be harmed,' said Hepesh. 'I give you my
word. We do not need you as hostages, if that is what
you're afraid of.'

Ssorg lumbered forward, and spoke to his master. 'Lord
Izlyr, let us take this one hostage in return for our safety.'

'Do not be so foolish,' Hepesh said haughtily. 'My men
hold the king prisoner. If I do not return with all of you
immediately, King Peladon will die. Is that what you
wish?'

The High Priest smiled cruelly. His remark had caused
consternation amongst the aliens. Then, without another
word, he turned on his heel and walked out. He knew
they would follow. They couldn't afford not to . . .


## I I

# The King's Avenger

From the depths of the tunnel ahead, the cry of Aggedor
rang out again. Grun stopped in his tracks. He had come
face to face with the Royal Beast once already in his life.
To survive a second time was surely tempting Fate too
far! The burly warrior gave a low growl of discourage-
ment. The Doctor turned and walked back to the awestruck King's Champion. Before the Doctor could speak,
Grun was pointing ahead and shaking his head vehemently. But the Doctor's voice was calm and reassuring. He
took the peculiar mirror device from his pocket, and
showed it to Grun.

'Grun, you're a brave warrior, I know,' he said. 'What you're going to see may amaze you—but trust me.'

Grun looked from the Doctor's confident face to the gleaming mirror, now still. What did it mean? Was this mad alien going to face the being that had so easily destroyed Torbis with nothing more deadly in his hand than a child's toy? He shook his grizzled head again, more uneasy still. Aggedor could be merciful to heroes, but to fools—never!

'It's alright, old chap,' insisted the Doctor. 'There's no need to get upset. This won't be as difficult as you think.' Then he added, under his breath, 'As long as Aggedor doesn't have too short a memory.'

But the Doctor could see that Grun wasn't going to be convinced. Then, as the warrior looked past him, jaw slack with fear, the Doctor knew the decision was no longer in their hands. At that awful, animal roar, the Doctor turned—to find Aggedor only yards away, rearing high above them, claws and tusks gleaming wickedly in the eerie phosphor light of the tunnel. It cried out again, and Grun dropped to his knees. Spreading his palms flat on the ground, the mighty warrior lowered his blood-caked forehead to the dusty earth in abject surrender. The Doctor stood firm.

'Now, Aggedor . . .' he said firmly, but in the crooning voice he had used when he and the monster had last met, 'you remember me, don't you?'

The great beast roared even louder, and advanced with a swift, shambling gait. Suddenly it slowed, halted and stood still, fascinated. The Doctor had started the hypno-disc spinning, and its spell was having an almost immediate effect . . . As the dancing flecks of light spun across the eyes of the monster, it stood swaying and softly purring. The only other sound was the Doctor's gentle crooning of the Venusian lullaby, its words incomprehensible but its power over the beast complete . . . Grun, expecting only a hideous death, felt nothing and looked up. First he glanced at the Doctor, and then at the beast which had once been so terrifying, and which was now purring with pleasure. It seemed unbelieveable! What was the magic in the toy that the Doctor held?

With Aggedor under control, the Doctor was able to look at his warrior companion. He smiled. Grun, too, was rapidly succumbing to the influence of the spinning disc.

'Grun!' the Doctor quietly commanded as he shielded the device from the King's Champion. 'Look away. Look at Aggedor!'

The pattern of light cut off from his fascinated eyes, Grun came back to reality, and looked at the Doctor with a new respect. What sort of a being was it who could defeat the greatest of the king's warriors in single-handed combat and subdue the Royal Beast without even a weapon in his hand? Paying no attention to the beast that had once threatened them, Grun suddenly knelt before the Doctor and placed his cropped head beneath the alien's hand. It was a dedication of the simplest kind, and the Doctor was both moved and pleased. He then insisted, having persuaded Grun to rise, on a more equal dedication, man to man. Extending his open hand, the Doctor clasped Grun's mighty wrist—and after a moment's hesitation, the warrior met his grasp with crushing power.

'I'm not your master, Grun,' declared the Doctor, 'but I'd be happy to be your friend. Blood brothers, as you might say.'

They smiled into each other's eyes, and a gentle roar from Aggedor seemed an apt comment on the Doctor's words. It also served to remind him of what they must next do.

'Aggedor is with us, Grun,' said the Doctor, and Grun, able now to control his fear, nodded in agreement. The Doctor moved to the friendly beast, and stroked its mighty neck. The hypnotic device was slipped back into his pocket, its work now done. 'You see, Grun, Aggedor isn't such a terrifying fellow after all. But I think we need him to convince Peladon—and his people—that Hepesh is the evil genius that could wreck their whole future, don't you?'

Grun nodded again, and gripped his sword, as though hungry for the chance to confront the High Priest. The

Doctor smiled, and indicated that he should put down his weapon. 'I don't think anybody will argue with us,' he said, with a nod towards Aggedor. 'Not with our friend here to accompany us! But we must move quickly—come!' And they started off along the tunnel that would take them into the heart of the Citadel of Peladon.

.    .    .    .    .

From his seat on the throne, Peladon saw Jo and the aliens enter, following Hepesh. He could make no move to greet them, however. The sword points that held his life in the balance were still poised at his throat, ready to act at the slightest sign of trouble. Hepesh studied the aliens and was satisfied from their reactions that they fully understood the danger of the situation. He smiled. Jo turned towards him, her eyes wide with concern for the young king. His face was pale, but otherwise showed no sign of fear. 'What are you going to do with him?' she demanded. 'He's done nothing to harm you. Let him go!'

'That is up to the delegates,' pointed out Hepesh. 'If they will cooperate . . .'

'You will answer to Federation justice,' hissed Izlyr fiercely. But he could do nothing.

'Your Federation has no jurisdiction over me or this planet,' corrected Hepesh. 'It is you that must answer to your superiors for your interference!'

Alpha Centauri, though far from brave, was prepared to defend his bureaucratic privileges to the letter of the law—within reason. 'You are holding us here by force. You will answer for that!'

Supremely confident, Hepesh gestured amiably at the soldiers which were scattered about the room. Apart from the two swords at the king's throat, all weapons were sheathed.

'I am not holding you,' replied the High Priest blandly. 'There are no swords or spears held against you. You came to this throne room at your own free will.'

'We didn't have much choice!' cried Jo, but Hepesh only gave her a cold glance before continuing.

'You are not wanted here, either as guests or hostages,' he said. 'I know the retribution this planet would suffer if any of you were harmed—so go in peace. Tell your masters that Peladon wants nothing of their Federation. But go—now!'

Hepesh had won. Or so it seemed to Jo and the aliens as they faced the defeated king in the silence that followed. A split second later, a series of terror-stricken shouts heralded the opening of the throne room doors with a mighty crash—and standing there were the Doctor, Grun . . . and Aggedor. The first reaction of Hepesh's men was to seize arms and attack the intruders—but at the sight of the Royal Beast, they dropped their weapons and fell to their knees in awe. Hepesh alone stood his ground. The two fanatics, now in a cold sweat of fear, continued to hold the king at point of death.

'Who dares to challenge Peladon of Peladon? Kneel and pay homage to his sacred guardian!' cried out the Doctor.

The tables were turned—but Hepesh was not beaten yet. The king was still his hostage, and he knew that Aggedor was no unearthly spirit. 'Do not listen to this alien heretic!' he cried. 'I am the High Priest of Aggedor and Regent to the kingdom of Peladon!'

'But you no longer speak for Aggedor, Hepesh!' the Doctor exclaimed. 'Aggedor stands by those who recognise the rightful king. Here is Grun, his Champion, as witness! And I condemn Hepesh as a traitor to his ruler, and to his sacred trust as guardian of the holy temple!' The Doctor paused, but Hepesh would not bow. He stood erect and haughty, eyes blazing in defiance. 'Be sensible,' said the Doctor quietly. 'You're beaten, Hepesh. Just surrender before anyone else gets killed.'

Hepesh gathered his cloak about him and strode forward, at the same time addressing his scornful words to the black helmets who so easily outnumbered the aliens. 'Do not believe his trickery!' he shouted, and moved amongst his men as though haranguing them into bravery. In fact, he had a purpose in his movements which was not made clear until he came close to the buttressed doorway. 'You know the aliens. Their machines and their magic do not fool us! The beast is not the Royal guardian—it is a common animal!' Suddenly he sprang to the wall and, seizing a flaming torch from its wall bracket, held it high. 'I will show you. It is a living monster, and not a holy spirit!'

Hepesh took a step towards Aggedor. The torch in his outstretched hand flared menacingly in the creature's face. A low growl of fear came from its shaggy throat. As the beast reared, the Doctor and Grun fell back. Rolling its head away from the threatening firebrand, Aggedor gave a fearsome howl. Hepesh lunged at it again, his face alight with cruel jubilation. 'I am its master!' he cried. 'When I command, it obeys!' Then, with a fierce gesture towards the Doctor, his voice rang out like the crack of a whip: 'Aggedor—kill!'

At the final thrust of flame, the great beast reared to its full height, its upraised claws thrashing the smoke-dim air. Then, with that terrifying howl of vengeance, it struck —but not at the Doctor. Brushing aside the torch as though it were a fly, the other mighty paw dealt a crushing blow on to Hepesh's bare head, and in an instant he was sprawled upon the bloodsoaked ground. Jo's scream died in her throat. The Doctor quickly brought out the hypno-disc and soothed the beast back into an uneasy calm. The black-helmeted temple troops prostrated themselves before the Royal Beast, and moaned in terror. It was the king who reached the fallen figure of Hepesh first, and he crouched low over him, cradling the dying old man in his arms. He wept openly.

Peladon knew that whatever the old priest had done, had been done for love of his people. There was only love and pity in his voice—not condemnation.

The old man opened his eyes. They were dark with pain. He spoke proudly, his failing voice reaching only the king's ears. 'I meant . . . to save our world . . .' the old man whispered. 'The old ways . . . perhaps I was wrong . .' He strained to look his young master in the eye for the last time, and his voice grew clearer for an instant. 'You

*are* the king. Rule wisely . . . my son. The future . . . that
you desire so greatly . . . will be yours . . .'

The proud head fell back. Gently, Peladon laid the limp
figure on the ground, and examined the old face, haughty
even in death. Then, closing the lifeless eyes, Peladon re
moved his royal cloak and covered the High Priest's body
with it lovingly.

The king stood up. The commander of the temple
guard, his sword and black helmet set aside, bowed his
knee before the ruler who held life and death in his hand.
Behind the commander, the two commandos who had
once held his life at their swordpoints knelt also. They
could expect nothing but Grun's sword upon their worth-
less necks, and the King's Champion strode forward to
carry out the task. But the king's hand checked him in his
stride. 'Sheath your sword, Grun. There will be no punish-
ments.' Peladon stepped to the throne and addressed all
those present in a voice which, though regal, was full of
deep emotion. A youth had become a man.

'Let the memory of this unhappy day be wiped from all
our chronicles,' declared the king. 'Let Hepesh the High
Priest be buried with the honour that his rank deserves.
He looked up at the tight group of silent aliens before him.
'For my sake, will the delegates attend?'

It was the Doctor who spoke. 'We honour your wisdom
and mercy, Peladon. These are the qualities that are
welcome within the Federation. Now, wear the crown of
Peladon.' His voice rang out, raising the hearts of every
one about him. 'Long live Peladon of Peladon— long live
the king!'

\* \* \* \* \*

The Federation treaty with Peladon awaited only the sig-
nature of the king. It would be given as part of the coronation ceremony—a supremely fitting overture to a glorious
reign. Although taking place barely days after the earlier
tragic events, the occasion had left Jo breathless with ex-
citement. Now, the Doctor was escorting her to the delegates' room—for a surprise, so he said.

'But what is it?' begged Jo, as the Doctor opened the door for her.

'See for yourself, Jo,' smiled the Doctor, delighted at the pleasure in Jo's eyes when she saw the familiar blue police box standing in the corner.

'The TARDIS!' exclaimed Jo, and ran over to it, as though to a long-lost friend. 'We've got it back—at last!'

'Yes,' murmured the Doctor smugly. 'Some of Peladon's lads heaved her back up the mountain for us.'

'Is she alright?' asked Jo, anxiously.

'Couldn't be better. Remember—I told you she was indestructible.'

'So we can really go home,' sighed Jo. 'Home to Earth.'

The Doctor looked at her thoughtfully, then pretended to take a closer look at the lock on the Tardis's door.

'Er . . . Jo . . .' he said, trying to sound casual. 'You do want to go back to Earth . . . don't you?'

Jo looked at him. He hadn't asked her the direct question, but she knew it was in his mind. Peladon had made it quite clear that once he was finally crowned king, he would make his request official. She could hardly ignore it then. She'd tried to find a way to explain, but how could she tell him the facts? She wasn't of his time or place. And, if she admitted the truth, she wasn't really cut out to be a queen, either. It was a super dream . . . but it could never be more than that.

'I wouldn't mind staying to see the coronation,' said Jo, brightly. 'Then we could go home . . .'

The Doctor looked relieved. 'Good idea, Jo,' he said, then beamed happily. 'You know . . . I haven't seen a good coronation since . . . oh, Queen Victoria!'

'Name dropper!' retorted Jo, and burst out laughing.

The Doctor opened the door leading to the corridor, and started to usher Jo out. 'To tell the truth,' he said with a dry chuckle, 'I think Izlyr could do with a bit of help to keep poor old Alpha Centauri calm.'

'Centauri's really looking forward to the coronation,' laughed Jo. 'Izlyr's getting quite worn out, coping with all those colour changes!' She started to go outside, but found herself held back by the Doctor's hand on her arm. She looked at him in surprise. He was listening intently to voices approaching from further along the castle corridor.

'Sshh, Jo . . . listen!'

Two of the voices they could hear were familiar: Izlyr and Alpha Centauri. But the other was that of a stranger —a woman. And a woman of considerable authority, by the sound of it. 'You say you are from Earth . . .' came the protesting whisper of the Martian warlord, 'but you are not expected!'

'And I keep telling you that I am the official Earth delegate!' boomed the female voice.

The shrill twitter of Alpha Centauri echoed hysterically. 'But you can't be! The Doctor is the accredited Earth delegate. He is our Chairman!'

'Doctor?' rang out the rich tones of the female intruder. 'What Doctor? Doctor who? Tell me!'

The Doctor and Jo looked at each other and shrugged sadly. It looked as though they were about to be found out.

'Pity about that,' murmured the Doctor. 'I'd've enjoyed seeing the crown on Peladon's head.'

'Me too,' agreed Jo. 'But I think we'd better go, don't you?'

The Doctor nodded, and produced a certain key from his pocket. 'Yes, Jo,' he said. 'I think we'd better . . .'

The doors of the Tardis had no sooner closed than the female Earth delegate entered in full glory, trailing Izlyr and Alpha Centauri in her resplendent wake.

'They should be here,' hissed the Martian. 'They will explain—' He never finished his sentence.

A bone-jarring, mechanical grinding noise filled the room. The lady Earth Delegate and Izlyr covered their ears. Alpha Centauri turned a particularly bright shade of mauve with the aural discomfort.

'What on Earth!' exclaimed Madam Chairman, finally managing to locate the source of the disagreeable noise. It was that ridiculous blue box . . . She blinked, and looked again, her mouth agape in almost comical amazement. The blue box had vanished completely.

# DOCTOR WHO

| | | |
|---|---|---|
| 0426114558 | TERRANCE DICKS<br>**Doctor Who and The**<br>**Abominable Snowmen** | £1.35 |
| 0426200373 | **Doctor Who and The**<br>**Android Invasion** | £1.25 |
| 0426201086 | **Doctor Who and The**<br>**Androids of Tara** | £1.25 |
| 0426116313 | IAN MARTER<br>**Doctor Who and The**<br>**Ark in Space** | £1.25 |
| 0426201043 | TERRANCE DICKS<br>**Doctor Who and The**<br>**Armageddon Factor** | £1.25 |
| 0426112954 | **Doctor Who and The**<br>**Auton Invasion** | £1.50 |
| 0426116747 | **Doctor Who and The**<br>**Brain of Morbius** | £1.35 |
| 0426110250 | **Doctor Who and The**<br>**Carnival of Monsters** | £1.25 |
| 042611471X | MALCOLM HULKE<br>**Doctor Who and**<br>**The Cave Monsters** | £1.50 |
| 0426117034 | TERRANCE DICKS<br>**Doctor Who and The**<br>**Claws of Axos** | £1.35 |
| 042620123X | DAVID FISHER<br>**Doctor Who and The**<br>**Creature from the Pit** | £1.25 |
| 0426113160 | DAVID WHITAKER<br>**Doctor Who and The Crusaders** | £1.50 |
| 0426200616 | BRIAN HAYLES<br>**Doctor Who and The Curse**<br>**of Peladon** | £1.50 |
| 0426114639 | GERRY DAVIS<br>**Doctor Who and The Cybermen** | £1.50 |
| 0426113322 | BARRY LETTS<br>**Doctor Who and The Daemons** | £1.50 |

Prices are subject to alteration

STAR Books are obtainable from many booksellers and newsagents. If you have any difficulty please send purchase price plus postage on the scale below to:-

Star Cash Sales
P.O. Box 11
Falmouth
Cornwall

OR

Star Book Service,
G.P.O. Box 29,
Douglas,
Isle of Man,
British Isles.

While every effort is made to keep prices low, it is sometimes necessary to increase prices at short notice. Star Books reserve the right to show new retail prices on covers which may differ from those advertised in the text or elsewhere.

**Postage and Packing Rate**
UK: 45p for the first book, 20p for the second book and 14p for each additional book ordered to a maximum charge of £1.63. BFPO and EIRE: 45p for the first book, 20p for the second book, 14p per copy for the next 7 books thereafter 8p per book. Overseas: 75p for the first book and 21p per copy for each additional book.